What's Wrong with Daddy?

Alida E. Young

*For the "young" Youngs—Ben, Eric, Betty,
Meredith, and Donovan*

*Special thanks to Barbara Fulmer, R.N., G.N.P.,
of the Alzheimer's Diagnostic Center
at Eisenhower Memorial Hospital and to the
Morongo Basin Alzheimer's Family Support Group.*

Cover photo by Bichsel Morris
Photographic Illustrators

Published by Willowisp Press, Inc.
401 E. Wilson Bridge Road, Worthington, Ohio 43085

Printed in the United States of America

10 9 8 7 6 5 4 3 2

ISBN 0-87406-066-4

One

JENNIFER Burke and her friend Caroline Powers stood under the pink and orange striped awning of the restaurant. Even in the shade it was hot. Jen adjusted the shopping bags in her arms and laughed. "I think we must have bought out all the stores in Southern California."

"Yeah, and wasn't it fun not to have our mothers tagging along saying, 'Dear, don't you think that's a little old for you?'"

Jen nodded. This was the first time she'd ever been allowed to choose her own summer clothes. Now that her mother had gone back to work, she didn't have time for shopping. "What time are we supposed to meet your mom?" Jen asked.

"We're early," Caroline said. "Let's go inside and get something cold to drink."

Jen followed her into The Carnival, a

favorite hangout of kids from Valley Academy, a private school specializing in music, drama, and dance. The Carnival had the best tacos in the entire San Fernando Valley. They ordered sodas and tacos at the counter. While they waited they waved to friends.

"Come on over to our booth," Mindy Wallace called.

"Thanks," Jen said, "But we've got too much junk."

They paid for their food, then slid into a booth with loud sighs and much groaning.

"Whew," Caroline said. "I'm beat. I didn't know shopping could be so tiring."

"It is when you buy out the stores. You're lucky to have two sets of parents. You get twice as much allowance." Jen had used all her birthday and baby-sitting money, and had borrowed her next three allowances. She had tried to talk her dad out of more money, but it was hard to argue with a lawyer. He always won—at home and in the courtroom.

Caroline was wadding her napkin into a hard little ball. "I'd trade the big allowance for parents like yours. Your family always has fun. You do everything together." She threw the napkin ball into Jen's lap and grinned. That was one of the things Jen liked best about her friend. She never stayed unhappy for very

4

long. "I can hardly wait for August fifteenth to get here," Caroline said, practically bouncing with excitement. "I'm sure glad your mom and dad invited me to go along on your vacation. Just think of all the neat things—water skiing, neat guys, boating, camping, neat guys. . . ."

Jen had been marking off the days on the calendar, just the way her father always did. It was sixty-six whole days before they would be heading up to Big Bear to try out the brand new eighteen-foot powerboat. That was practically forever.

Caroline fished through some of her packages and dug out a bathing suit. "Do you really think this red two-piece looked good on me? I sort of wish I'd bought the yellow."

"You looked great in both of them. With your dark hair and eyes you can wear red and yellow. I'm surprised you didn't buy both."

"Yeah, that's what Mom does." Caroline grinned. "Then she returns one. Stores hate to see my mother coming."

"Next time we shop, maybe your mom would take us to downtown Los Angeles. Everybody says you can get great bargains in the garment district."

Caroline whispered, "Don't look now, but I think those two guys in the next booth are staring at you."

5

Jen tried to sneak a look at the boys across the aisle. She didn't recognize them.

Caroline made a face. "I don't know why I had to pick a best friend who looks like you do. Everybody stares at your blue eyes and that tan. School's only been out a week and you already have a super tan."

"I'm just lucky I take after my dad," Jen said. "We both tan easily. Anyway, you're cute. Everybody says so. And I wish I had your dimple."

"Great. My only claim to fame is a dimple that only shows when I smile. Why do you think I go around with this stupid grin plastered on my face?" Caroline asked.

"Don't worry. Mom says thirteen is the worst age to be."

"Yeah, next year we'll be gorgeous," Caroline said doubtfully.

"Speaking of gorgeous. Did I tell you who Mom's working with?" Caroline shook her head. "Tod Hawthorne! Can you believe it? He's only the hottest soap star in town. It's his first TV movie."

"Can your mom get us on the set?"

"No. I already asked." Jen liked having her mother work as an assistant director for a production company. The company made movies for cable and network television.

Sometimes Jen could visit the set and take a friend with her.

"You talk about me being lucky. You're the lucky one, Jen. You have a mother who works with famous people and a father who looks like a movie star."

Jennifer's friends all thought her dad was "darling." And Jen had to admit it was fun when people asked him for his autograph. Six-foot-two, trim, light brown curly hair, and blue eyes—he looked a bit like a younger Paul Newman.

Jen glanced at her watch. "Shouldn't your mom be here by now?" she asked.

"My mother is always late."

They both began to gather their packages together.

"Hey, Jen, which sack has the blue blouse I'm borrowing for tomorrow?"

"What blue blouse? I didn't buy a blue blouse."

"I know that. I'm talking about the one I asked you to bring along. I mean, I asked your dad. Didn't he give you the message?"

Jen shook her head. "I'm sorry. Dad's just so darned busy right now. You can get it when you drop me off."

"Hi, Caroline."

They both looked up to see a tall boy in

7

white shorts and white knit shirt smiling down at them. Suddenly Jen felt rumpled and hot and grungy.

"Gary. Hi," Caroline said.

"Did you leave anything in the stores?" he asked and nodded at the packages.

"Not much. Jen, you haven't met Gary Sivert. Gary, this is my best friend, Jennifer Burke."

"I'm glad to meet you, Jennifer Burke."

He smiled at Jen, and she felt her face flush. You'd think by age thirteen you wouldn't blush every time you meet a good-looking boy, she thought. And he was good looking. He had dark curly hair, dark brown, almost black eyes, and a smile that made you feel good.

"I haven't seen you playing tennis lately," Caroline said to him.

"I don't have much spare time right now," he said. "My grandparents are staying with us for a while." He nodded at the bag in his arms. "This is chicken. My granddad loves fried drumsticks." He smiled at Jen again. "Do you play tennis?"

"Does she play tennis!" Caroline said. "Next to her dad, she has the best lob in the neighborhood."

"Burke—David Burke—is he your dad?"

Jen smiled and nodded. She was pleased

8

that Gary knew who her father was.

"I've seen him play at the country club. He's good enough to be a pro," Gary said.

"He could have been a tennis pro, or a performer. But law school won out."

"Why haven't I seen you at the club?" Gary asked.

"I guess you weren't looking my way," Jen answered. "I go sometimes, but I usually play at the court in Lakeside Park."

"I'm free in the morning about ten. Do you two want to play a couple of sets? I can bring a friend for doubles."

Jen and Caroline exchanged glances. "You bet," Caroline said.

"Sure," Jen said casually, but inside she was about to burst with excitement. "We'll be there."

"Well, guess I'd better get this chicken home before it's cold. My granddad likes to eat early. See you tomorrow."

When he was out of hearing range, Jen said, "You're a rat for not telling me about him."

"He's a friend of my sister's, so he must be fifteen or sixteen. I figured he'd never look at us. Betty says he's really nice, though."

"Nice" wasn't usually a word Jen liked to use to describe a really neat guy. But there was something warm and friendly and nice about him, like the way he had spoken about her dad. It always made her feel good when people praised her father.

"Caroline? Jennifer?"

It was Mrs. Powers waving to them from the door. "Come on, girls. I'm double parked."

Mrs. Powers stopped in front of Jen's house. "Mom, I have to go in and get a blouse from Jen."

"We don't have time," Caroline's mother said. "Your father is picking you up in half an hour."

"Nuts! I forgot. I like seeing Dad, but I can't stand those brats."

Caroline's father had married a woman with three kids. Caroline was always griping about them. Jen thought it might be fun to have some brothers and sisters.

"Jen, I'll call you when I get back," Caroline said. "Okay?"

"Sure. And thanks for taking us to the mall, Mrs. Powers. Bye."

As Jen walked up to the porch, she was surprised to see her father's car in the circular drive. He never came home this early.

The front door was unlocked. After the bright sunlight, it took Jen's eyes a few minutes to adjust to the dark room. "Dad?"

She heard banging in her father's study. "Daddy, it's me."

Her father charged out of the study. "Jenny, have you seen my briefcase?"

"No. Didn't you take it to work?"

"I don't know why people move my things. I have an important appointment, and I need that briefcase."

No wonder he looked so distracted and harried, Jen thought as she set her packages on the dining room table.

"This hasn't been my day." He ran his fingers through his hair and began looking in drawers and cupboards. "Help me find it, Jenny."

They searched the kitchen and family room. Then they tried the study again.

"I'll never make it in time. I have to be downtown by—uh—right away." He slumped down at his desk. "I guess I'd better cancel the appointment."

He flipped through his phone number file several times. "Nothing is ever where it's supposed to be!"

Jen had never seen him so agitated before. He was usually the calm, cool member of the family. Her mother was the impatient one who never sat still.

Jen came over to the desk and put her arm

around his neck. Something bad must have happened to get him so upset that he couldn't find the number to his own office. She knew it by heart. "Here, let me get it for you." She laughed. "I'll be your secretary."

"I'm quite capable of . . . I'm sorry, honey. I didn't mean to snap at you." He gave her a hug and kissed her cheek. "Thanks. You call in for me and say I'm sick. I'm going to soak in the hot tub, then lie down for a while."

Jen watched him go out to the spa. Ever since he'd been in the hospital with pneumonia in the spring, he hadn't seemed like himself. She hoped he wasn't getting sick again.

☆　☆　☆　☆　☆

That night after dinner, Jen modeled her new clothes. Her mom and dad both praised her for her good taste. Jennifer and her father swam for a while, then got into their terry robes. Her dad seemed perfectly fine. He made popcorn, a Friday night ritual in her family.

Jennifer loved the family room with the lights down low. The rest of the colonial style house was furnished with Early American antiques that her mother had brought from

Massachusetts. But her dad had decorated the family room with oriental furniture. The room had lots of plants and an aquarium filled with exotic fish.

Jen lay on the thick sea-green carpet with her arms under her head. Her dad sat on the low sofa, and her mom stretched out with her head in his lap. He started juggling popcorn, deliberately dropping the kernels into her mouth.

In between bites Jen's mother tried to talk. "Did I tell you Craig Shelley is interested in my play, *Death Is No Angel*?"

"Only about five times," her dad said with a big grin. "I know he'll produce it. Didn't I tell you it's the best thing you've ever written? Sweetheart, you're going to be famous someday."

Her mother had quit her job when Jen was born. During those thirteen years she'd written a dozen screen plays, but none had ever been produced.

"Anybody else want lemonade?" Jen asked as she started for the kitchen. No one answered. She turned around to see her parents kissing. Caroline said her folks never hugged or kissed in front of her and her sister. Maybe that was why the Powers' were divorced.

When Jen came back with her drink, her

father was playing an old folk song on his guitar. Jen went over to the spinet and accompanied him while her mother sang. Jen hadn't wanted to take piano lessons, but now she was glad she could play. The big concert grand was in the living room, but Jen liked the small piano better because her father had bought it just for her.

"David, I wish you two would play something besides folk songs and ballads," her mother said.

Jen's father stood up and went into his Elvis impression of "You Ain't Nothin' But a Hound Dog."

Jen's mother clapped and laughed. "David, you're crazy."

"Oh, you don't like Elvis? Well, how about this?"

He began to play Hawaiian music, and all three of them tried to outdo each other dancing the hula. The evening went so fast, it was bedtime before Jen knew it.

She kissed both her parents and reluctantly went up to her room. What a wonderful day it had been. Caroline was right. I am the luckiest person in the world.

Two

THE next morning Jen got up at seven as usual to go jogging with her father. But he wasn't downstairs or outside. Maybe he's sleeping in, she thought. Her mother often slept late, but her dad hardly ever did.

Jen went back to her room to decide what she should wear to play tennis with Gary. Her blue and white tennis dress was getting too short, but it still looked good on her.

When her dad wasn't up at eight o'clock, Jen went ahead and showered and dressed. She pulled a wide blue band around her thick, sun-streaked blonde hair and put on some lip gloss. Not bad, she thought. I look fifteen—well, almost.

She fixed herself a breakfast of orange juice, yogurt with fresh strawberries and granola, and toasted whole grain bread. Her dad insisted she eat a good breakfast to make up for the junk food she ate the rest of the day.

She was just putting her dishes in the dishwasher when her mother came downstairs. Jen couldn't help grinning as her mother fumbled at the refrigerator with half-opened eyes. Her mom was definitely not a morning person.

"Is Dad okay?" Jen asked.

Her mother turned sharply. "Why do you ask?"

"He never misses our Saturday morning jog. And yesterday he had me call the office to say he was sick."

"He's fine. He had a bad night. He couldn't sleep."

"I hope he isn't going to get sick again and have to go to the hospital."

"No, he's just been working too hard. Where are you headed this morning?"

"Playing tennis," Jen said. And just then she realized that Caroline wouldn't be at the park this morning. She'd be with her father.

"Be back by lunchtime. I have to get a haircut and do some shopping. Your father forgot to take the weekly cleaning. Now, I don't have anything to wear to the Shelleys' party tonight. I hope I can buy something decent."

"Is it okay if I ask some kids over to swim in

the pool this afternoon?" Jen asked.

"I guess so. Your dad will be here."

Jen picked up her racket and canvas bag and headed for the back door. She hesitated. "Mom? Are you sure Dad's okay? He was really upset about something yesterday."

"Oh, it's just a case he's working on. It's nothing to worry about. Have fun, honey."

☆　☆　☆　☆　☆

Jen enjoyed the short walk to the park. The neighborhood was pretty, with large houses and lots of flowers and shrubs. Palm trees and eucalyptus lined the curving street. It wasn't as fancy as Beverly Hills or Bel Aire, but sometimes you saw a movie or TV star out jogging or shopping at the supermarket. And it was handy for her mother. The studio where she worked was only a few miles away.

At the park she found Gary waiting for her on a bench under a palm.

"Hi," he said. "Sorry, I didn't bring a friend. But I see you're alone, too. What happened to Caroline?"

"She forgot she was to spend the weekend with her dad. I hope you don't mind."

"Heck, no. I like singles better, anyhow. All the courts are full. Want to do something else for a while or just talk?" he asked.

Jen dropped her things on the bench and sat down. "Let's talk. If we leave the area we'll never get a court."

Neither one said anything for a moment, then they both spoke at once. "Which school do you go to?" Jen asked. "How long have you been playing tennis?" Gary wanted to know.

They laughed. Then both answered at once. "Since I was six," Jen said. "Valley High. Tenth grade," Gary answered.

They both hesitated again. "This is getting ridiculous," Gary said quickly. "We need signals."

"Or maybe we should raise our hands before speaking."

"I have a good idea. Since we both want to know about each other, let's give a brief biographical sketch. You know, like on the dust jacket of a book. Ladies first."

"Well . . . there's nothing very interesting about me. I'm thirteen, going on fourteen"—in eleven months, she thought to herself—"and I'm five-foot-five"—if I stand up very straight and stretched. "Dad says I'll be five-nine at least. I go to Valley Academy. I like music, especially piano, swimming, tennis, water skiing, books, movies, and trivia games. My favorite colors are blue and lavendar. My favorite flower is a lilac. I love Chinese food and German chocolate cake. I'm good in literature and history and awful at math. And I want to be a lawyer like my dad some day," she said almost in one breath. "Now, it's your turn."

"I knew when I met you yesterday that we would have a lot in common. I like all the sports you said, except I've never water skied. My favorite color—on a girl—is blue. I can eat more Chinese food than anybody I know. I love books. I want to be a writer—and a court just opened. Hurry up!"

Gary grabbed Jen's hand and drew her to her feet. She picked up her racket, and they ran to the empty court.

They volleyed for a few minutes. "Okay," Gary said. "Are you ready to get whipped?"

"Whipped? Ha! I told you I've been playing since I was six."

"Would you believe three?" he asked.

Instead of answering, she served a blistering ball just inside the center line for an easy ace. Then she gave him a pretend smirk.

They played two sets. He won both, but by the narrowest of margins. "Want to play another?" he asked.

"It's getting too hot. Anyway, I'm supposed to be home for lunch. Would you like to come with me?" Jen asked. "We can have lunch and swim in the pool. You could meet my dad. Now, he's a really good tennis player."

"You're plenty good for—"

"If you say, 'for a girl,' I'll belt you one."

"I was going to say, for someone who's only been playing since she was six."

"Hmm. . .Why don't I believe that?" Jen asked. "Well, do you want to come home with me? It won't be fancy. We just have sandwiches and salad on Saturdays."

"It sounds great. I don't have to be home until two-thirty."

"Come on. I'll race you," Jen said.

He groaned. "Do you always have this much energy?"

"You should try keeping up with my dad. It takes plenty of energy."

"I have to meet this man. He sounds like Superman."

"He believes in keeping fit. He's forty-two, but he looks lots younger."

☆ ☆ ☆ ☆ ☆

When they got to Jen's house, they found her father stretched out, face down, on a lounge by the pool.

"Dad? I'm home."

Her father turned over, raised up, and shaded his eyes with his hand. He was unshaven and looked every minute of his forty-two years. For a second he seemed a bit dazed, then he smiled. "Oh, it's you, Jenny. I guess I must have dozed off." He nodded to Gary. "Hello—sorry, your name escapes me."

"This is Gary Sivert, Dad. You've never met him."

Gary held out his hand. "I'm really glad to meet you, sir. I just now realized that I saw you when I was about nine. I was in the hospital. I'd just had my tonsils out. You did a show in the children's ward. You made my throat hurt from laughing so hard."

"Sorry," he said, looking pleased. "Guess I'll have to try not to be funny."

"We played tennis this morning," Jen said. "Gary's good. He beat me two sets."

"Looks like you're going to have to practice harder," her father said. "Jenny, your mother's already gone shopping. She said everything's in the refrigerator for lunch." He turned to Gary. "You are staying for lunch, aren't you?"

"Yes, sir. Thank you."

Jen couldn't believe how polite Gary was. Not many of the kids she knew called people sir, except for Bill Woodrow next door who was in the Marines.

"You two talk while I bring our lunch out here," Jen said, and headed for the kitchen. At the door she stopped to look at her father. It wasn't like him to go unshaven. She almost wished she hadn't invited Gary home. The two were talking about tennis. Her father got off the lounge, picked up Gary's racket, and began demonstrating a serve. She smiled to herself, surprised to realize how much she wanted Gary to like her father.

Jen brought out the plates of fresh fruit salad and the tuna sandwiches her mother had prepared. She set them on the patio table. "Okay, come and get it."

Gary came over, but her father headed for the house. "You two go ahead and eat," he said. "I had a late breakfast. If you need me, I'll be in the study working on a brief."

Gary was quiet while they ate. "Your dad sure knows his tennis. He really helped me with my serve."

"He's always after me about throwing the ball too high," Jen said. "Does your dad play tennis?"

"His game's golf. I kid him about riding around in a golf cart."

"What does he do for a living?"

"Sivert's Insurance Agency. Mom keeps the books. They both work long hours."

"I think my dad has been working too hard." She lapsed into silence, thinking about him. No matter what her mother had said, Jen knew something was wrong.

When they finished eating, Gary helped Jen clean up the dishes. He looked around the huge colonial style kitchen with its fireplace and sideboards. "This is really nice."

Jen wiped her hands on a towel. "Come on. I'll show you the rest of the house."

She took him on a tour. "Wow, what a huge place," Gary said with awe. "How many fireplaces are there?"

"Five." Jen laughed. "Kind of silly for Southern California, isn't it? But Mom wanted a house just like the one she grew up in back east."

"I wish our place were larger, especially now that my grandparents are living with us. Do you have any other family?"

"No. My dad's parents died when he was little. I don't even get to see my mom's folks but about twice a year."

On their way back outside, they passed the study. They could hear her father playing his guitar, repeating over and over the same few bars.

Gary smiled sympathetically. "You should hear me. I'm trying to learn the accordian.

23

Grandma says I sound like Smokey the Bear with emphysema."

Jen didn't tell him that her father was an excellent guitarist. "Come on," she said brightly, "let's swim." Her voice sounded forced and high to her own ears.

Gary glanced quickly at her, then looked at his watch. "Jennifer, I should get home. I have to take care of my grandfather this afternoon."

"Is he sick?"

"Well, someone has to be with him all the time. I hope you don't mind."

Jen could still hear the awful sound of her father playing the same notes. "No, I don't mind."

"Thanks for the games and lunch. I really had a good time today."

"Me, too," Jen said. Gary got his racket, and Jen let him out the front door. "Bye, Gary."

Jen watched him run down the walk to the street. He stopped, turned to look back, and waved.

"Good-bye," she said softly. With a long sigh, she closed the front door. She could hardly wait to tell Caroline about Gary. A tenth grader had actually treated her like a person. She realized she was smiling broadly and was glad no one could see her.

She passed the study again. It was quiet now. Often her father played his stereo while he worked, but not a sound came from the room.

☆　☆　☆　☆　☆

Jen was in the pool when Rosita Gomez arrived at six o'clock. Rosita cleaned house, cooked meals, did the laundry, and stayed all night whenever Jen's parents were going to be out late. Juan Gomez took care of the yard and pool, and did odd jobs like fixing dripping faucets.

"Hi, Rosita." Jen waved. "Come on in. The water's great."

"Not today. Your mama wants me to take up the hem on her new dress."

Jen floated on her back. The weekends that Caroline stayed at her father's were a real bore. Saturday nights she and Caroline usually took turns sleeping over at each other's house.

"Jen," Rosita called, "get ready for dinner."

Jen climbed out of the pool, rinsed off in the outside shower, and put on her terry robe. She hurried inside, anxious to see what Rosita had fixed for dinner. Tonight there were refried beans, enchiladas, and red Mexican rice.

She and Rosita were in the kitchen eating

when they heard Jen's mother shouting. They could hear her over the sound of the stereo in the study across the hall. "David! It's getting late. We're supposed to be at the Shelleys' by eight."

The stereo switched off. Her dad answered, "For what?"

Her mom's voice was sharp. "We're having dinner there tonight. Did you conveniently forget?"

"I didn't forget! I just don't feel like going."

Jen stared at her plate, unable to look at Rosita. She was embarrassed that her parents were arguing.

"Honey, you know how important this is to me," her mother was saying.

"I know it's important to you. So go ahead without me."

"I don't want to go by myself. It's a dinner. You'll louse up the seating arrangement."

"And that would be a terrible tragedy, wouldn't it?" he said sarcastically.

"Please, David."

"Oh, all right!"

Jen heard the door slam and her father's feet stomping across the hardwood floors and up the stairs. In a few minutes he yelled down, "Ellen? Where the devil are my blue socks?"

"I assume they're in the top drawer of the

dresser where Rosita always puts them. Please hurry, Dave. They are going to be eating dessert by the time we get there."

Her mother headed for the stairs. Jen heard her muttering, "Men! They couldn't find their noses if they weren't attached."

Suddenly Jen's enchilada no longer tasted good. "Rosita, I think I'll put my plate in the fridge and eat later. I'm not as hungry as I thought I was."

"It's all right, *querida.* And don't worry. You should hear Juan and me yelling at each other."

"But my mom and dad hardly ever argue, let alone yell."

"So, maybe yelling is good. It gets out the bad feelings, like lancing a boil gets out the poisons." She patted Jen's shoulder. "After I clear up the dishes, how about a game of Trivial Pursuit?"

"Okay," Jen said. She didn't really want to play, but she hated to hurt Rosita's feelings.

They were playing on the dining room table when Jen's parents were ready to leave for the party. No one would guess her parents had been yelling at each other earlier. Maybe Rosita was right about an argument clearing the air. As they came down the curved staircase arm in arm, her father was singing

"Steppin' Out With My Baby."

Jen's mom and dad came into the archway of the dining room and posed.

"Oh, Mom, you look beautiful," Jen said. The new jade green dress made her mother's eyes seem even greener.

Rosita clapped her hands. "You two look like movie stars going to a big premiere."

"Jeeves, my good man, bring round the limousine," her dad said, using a phoney English accent.

"Much as I love all this admiration," her mother said, "we have to go." She kissed Jen on the forehead. "We'll probably be late."

"Have fun," Jen called as they left.

Rosita and Jen finished their game. Jen was tired and went to bed early. She couldn't have been asleep long when she was awakened by her parents' loud voices. They were home from the party, and they obviously hadn't had fun.

"How could you possibly forget Barbara Shelley's first name?" her mother was asking.

"I refuse to call anyone Babsy."

"You embarrassed me to death tonight."

"I just told the truth. I said she ought to go back to the fat farm."

"Were you deliberately trying to make me look bad? Don't you want Craig to produce my play? That's it, isn't it? You're jealous that I might be successful, aren't you?"

"That's not it at all." Her father's voice sounded tired. "Let's not fight, Ellie. I'm really beat."

Although the night was warm, Jen pulled the covers over her head so she couldn't hear any more.

Jen lay awake for a long time. She wished she could call Caroline, but it was much too late. Hungry now, she picked up her pencil flashlight. She slipped quietly out of her room and down the stairs to the kitchen. The full moon was so bright she didn't need a light. The cold enchiladas and beans didn't look appetizing, so she dished up a huge bowl of butter brickle ice cream.

Jen sat in one of the kitchen rockers, remembering when she was little. Every night her dad had rocked her to sleep. Now, the squeaking of the chair seemed comforting.

Jen finished the ice cream and rinsed her dish. She was headed back upstairs when she saw her father pacing the length of the living room. Back and forth, back and forth he paced, like one of the caged tigers at the zoo. She started to speak to him, then changed her mind. There was something frightening about the way he was pacing. She crept silently up the stairs and back to bed.

The next morning, she called Caroline as early as she dared. Caroline finally came to the phone. "Hang on while I carry the phone into the closet," Caroline whispered. "There's no privacy in this place."

Caroline started right in complaining about her new stepfamily. "I hate it here, Jen. This place is a madhouse. The two little boys are creeps, and the girl is awful. And Phyllis is a slob. I don't know how my dad could have left Mom for somebody like her."

Jen was interested in Caroline's problems, but she didn't want to hear about them right now. "Caroline? How did your dad act before—before he left your mom?"

"He wasn't home much. And when he was, they were yelling at each other."

Jen's heart sank to her stomach.

"Hey, I have to go. One of the little twerps is yanking on the phone cord. I'll call you as soon as I get home."

Jen heard a loud crash. The line went dead . . . as dead as Jen suddenly felt inside. She sat there holding the receiver until the dial tone sounded, then she replaced it. Oh, please, God, don't let them get a divorce. I don't want to be like Caroline with two sets of parents. She doubled her hands into fists. I love Mom, but I won't live with anybody but Daddy.

Three

BY afternoon, Jen felt foolish for having thought her parents might get divorced. Everybody was in a wonderful mood. Rosita had fixed a huge brunch of ham and eggs, waffles, and strawberries with gobs of whipped cream. Her father had eaten everything without once complaining about fat and cholesterol.

When Rosita was leaving, she whispered to Jen, "Didn't I tell you everything was all right?"

She hugged Rosita. "I know. I was a jerk."

After everybody read the Sunday paper, Jen and her mom and dad swam. Then they played a game of Scrabble, which her mother won.

Caroline phoned late in the afternoon. Jen took the call in the kitchen. "Hi," she said. "Why don't you come over? We're going to have a barbeque on the patio."

"Wish I could. But after I've been at Dad's, my mother gets into all this maternal garbage. I'll come over after breakfast tomorrow. Usually her motherly binges only last one day."

"Let's play some tennis," Jen suggested. "I need to practice."

"Hey, I forgot. We were supposed to meet Gary and his friend at the park yesterday. What did you do?"

"He came alone, too. Oh, Caroline, he's wonderful. He's so easy to talk to. We played two sets, then we had lunch together at my house. Can you believe it? A tenth grader!"

"You lucky dog, having all that fun while I was going bananas at my dad's house. Hey, but what were all those questions about this morning? You sounded upset."

"Oh, I was letting my imagination get away from me just because my mom and dad had a fight."

"You mean they had a real fight?" Caroline whispered. "Did he hit your mom like Kathy Freeman's dad did?"

"No! My father would never hit anybody," Jen said, indignant at the very idea. "It was just an argument."

"Good! It would be awful if your parents split up. We'd never get to see each other."

"I'm not worried about it any more," Jen said. But a little worm of fear had buried itself in her mind.

☆　☆　☆　☆　☆

Jen was counting the money she'd earned from teaching the neighbor's three grandkids to swim. They had paid her twenty-five dollars for each of the kids.

Jen's mother came into the kitchen with a clipboard. "Well, what are you going to do with all those riches?"

"I might make a down payment on some new water skis."

Her mother sat in the rocker. "You know, you're very good with children. You can probably earn more money that way."

"I had a terrible time," Jen said. "All the kids wanted to do was play with Daddy. You should have seen him. He pretended to be a talking sea monster with the flu."

Jen's mother smiled and shook her head. "All children seem to love your father," she said, almost as if to herself.

Jen folded her money and went over to the calendar to mark off another day. Big Bear, here we come. Then she noticed that Friday, June 27, was circled. For a second she couldn't think why that date was marked. Then she remembered. It was her mom and dad's fifteenth wedding anniversary.

At the back of the calendar was a list of gifts for each year of marriage. Crystal was listed for the fifteenth. Crystal was expensive. But seventy-five dollars ought to buy something nice, she thought.

"Mom?"

"Mmm?" her mother said without looking up from her script.

"Mom, what are you and daddy going to do on your anniversary?"

"Oh, we'll probably go out to dinner. Maybe we'll see a movie."

"Oh." Jen was disappointed that she wasn't included. She knew it was silly. Anniversaries were for the married couple, not their kids.

Her mother was looking at her. "I have a better idea," she said. "Your father hates to eat out. How would you like it if we ordered Chinese food, a really gourmet, eleven-course meal?"

"Daddy would like that, wouldn't he? And I can fix the dessert. Oh, Mom, it'll be fun."

☆　☆　☆　☆　☆

On the twenty-seventh, just as soon as her

34

parents left for work, Jen called Caroline. "Come on over. The coast is clear."

Jen was mixing the cake when Caroline came to the back door. Her arms were loaded with the decorations and gifts that Jen had bought and left at Caroline's house. With the money from the swimming lessons, Jen had bought streamers and paper lanterns, a beautiful crystal unicorn for her mother's collection, and a small crystal paperweight for her father's desk. They looked like plain old glass to Jen, but the salesclerk had assured her they were genuine crystal.

When the cake was in the oven and the timer was set, Jen and Caroline started decorating the living room. They rolled up all the rugs. Then they got so carried away sliding on the waxed floors that they didn't hear the timer go off.

Jen smelled the cake burning. "Oh, no!"

She rushed to the kitchen and burned her fingers taking the overdone cake out of the oven. "It's ruined!" she wailed.

"It's not so bad," Caroline said. "My mom's cakes look like that all the time. She just cuts off the burnt edges and uses globs of frosting on those spots."

"But I want everything to be perfect."

"Nobody will notice."

While the cake cooled, Jen and Caroline strung crepe paper and lanterns in the living room. In one corner Jen spread out a Chinese shawl and three large cushions.

"What's that for?" Caroline asked.

"That's where we're going to eat. Then after I light the candles on the cake, I'll play Mom and Dad's song. They're going to dance to it."

"Wow, that really sounds romantic."

"It's going to be wonderful."

☆ ☆ ☆ ☆ ☆

Jen's mother arrived home first with all the Chinese food.

"If Daddy's late, it's going to get cold," Jen said.

"It'll warm up just fine in the microwave. Is the table all set?"

"I have a surprise for you in the living room," Jen said, trying to hide her excitement. "It's okay if we eat in there, isn't it. I even have chopsticks laid out."

"That sounds fine, honey. I'm going up and take a shower. It's been a hectic day."

"Mom, would you and Daddy wear the Chinese robes you got in Hawaii?"

"I will, but you may have trouble getting your dad into his."

36

Jen made a last minute check of everything. The living room looked great. The cake was a little lopsided, but not too noticeable. Jen glanced at herself in the hall mirror. She didn't have a Chinese robe, so she had put on pajama bottoms and a jacket with a dragon on the back.

Her father was nearly an hour late getting home. Jen kept going to the front window to watch for his car. When he finally drove in, Jen ran out to meet him. "Hurry, Daddy, the food's getting cold. And I have a surprise for you and Mom."

He gave her a hug. "Slow down, Jenny. I'm going to soak in the hot tub for a few minutes," her father said. "The traffic was a mess. Everybody in the Los Angeles basin must be headed out of town for the weekend."

"Don't take too long. And will you wear your Chinese robe?" He made a face. "Please."

He tweaked her nose. "How can I resist that super sad look?" They walked into the house together, with Jen carrying his briefcase.

"Mom," she called. "Dad's here."

While Jen waited for her parents to get ready, she removed the wire handles from the cartons of Chinese food and set them in the microwave oven. She was sneaking a fried shrimp just as they came into the kitchen.

"Oh, you both look wonderful," she said with her mouth full.

"Any mail?" her father asked.

"Just junk mail mostly. There's one that looks like the income tax refund, though. It's on your desk," Jen said.

"It's about time," he said. "I sent that in—well—a long time ago."

"David, you didn't get it off until the very last minute. Remember? I kept bugging you about it."

"I don't know what you're talking about. I never put off things to the last minute," he said sharply.

As he headed into the study, Jen wished she hadn't mentioned the tax return until after the party. Still, it would put him in a better mood. Even after the soak in the hot tub, he seemed tired.

Jen and her mother were ready to dish up the food, but her father was still in the study. "You'd better go drag him out of there, Jen. I'll fix the jasmine tea."

Jen hurried across the hall to the study to find her father working furiously with his calculator. "Come on, Daddy, dinner's ready."

"I never make mistakes. They're wrong. Some computer probably went crazy!"

"Daddy, please. It's time for the party."

"What's the matter with this stupid calculator! Cheap junk never works right." His voice was high and agitated, almost yelling.

Jen's mother came to the door. "What's wrong, Dave?"

"The IRS says we owe them. They claim I made an error in math!"

"Let me see," she said.

"No!" He picked up the calculator again, but after a moment he threw it on the desk. He pressed his hands to his temples. "I'll work on it tomorrow. My eyes are bothering me. I hope I don't need glasses."

Jen gave her mother a worried look and could see the same worry on her mother's face.

"As you said, it's probably just a computer error. Come on, let's see what kind of surprise Jen has for us."

"Both of you close your eyes," Jen said. "No peeking."

She took their arms and led them to the living room archway. "Now, you can look."

"Oh, it's beautiful," her mother said.

Her father hugged her. "You really outdid yourself, kitten."

"Caroline helped me decorate. I made the dessert all by myself, though. Now, you two sit down on those cushions, and I'll serve you."

☆ ☆ ☆ ☆ ☆

Everybody ate until they were almost too full to move. Jen's father seemed relaxed and happy. "It's time for my presents," Jen said. Her parents always opened their presents to each other at midnight.

Jen handed them the gifts and watched excitedly. Her mother tore off the wrappings. Her father, as usual, opened his carefully, so he wouldn't tear the paper.

"Oh, honey, a unicorn!" Her mother kissed her. "I love it."

Her father picked up the paperweight and held it to the light. "Look at the colors. It's like a prism." He stared at it for a long time as if hypnotized.

"Do you like it?" Jen asked. "It's supposed to be real crystal."

He leaned over and kissed Jen. "I'll treasure it always." He rolled it around and around with his fingers. "Wherever I am, it will remind me of you."

"Now, for the surprise," Jen went to the piano and sat down at the bench. With a flourish, she ran her fingers over the keys. Then she began to play "The Anniversary Song."

"You two are supposed to dance now," Jen said.

Jen's father helped her mother to her feet. Her mother slipped into her father's arms. He sang the words. "Oh, how we danced on the night we were wed...."

Jen sighed as she watched them dance cheek to cheek. Caroline was right. It was romantic. At the end of the song, they kissed. Then, hand in hand, they came over to the piano.

"Thank you for the surprise," they both said together.

"Has anybody got room for cake?" Jen asked.

"I always have room for a cake you've baked," her dad answered.

"Wait here. I'll be right back."

In the kitchen Jen lit the fifteen candles and carried the cake to the living room. She moved slowly so the candles wouldn't blow out.

At the archway, she stopped. "Ta da! Happy anniversary. May you have a hundred more."

She set the cake on the large marble-topped coffee table where she'd put the plates and forks. "Come over here," she said. "Daddy, you cut the first piece."

Her father sat on the couch. He picked up the silver cake knife. As he started to cut the cake, his hand began to shake. The knife clattered onto the table.

"I hate chocolate cake," he said.

At first Jen thought he was teasing. She grinned at him. "Daddy, you know it's your favorite."

But he wasn't teasing. He stood up.

"Daddy, I know it doesn't look very good. It got a little burnt, and I had to cut off the edges, but it'll taste—"

"The smell of it makes me sick!" He charged out of the room.

"Daddy!"

Jen started after him, but her mother stopped her. "Leave him alone, honey."

She blinked back tears. Why was he so angry? "Mom, what did I do wrong?" she asked, trying to keep from crying.

"You didn't do anything wrong. It was a wonderful party. Your father's just working too hard. He'll be all right once he's had his vacation."

But Jen knew something was terribly wrong. He had never spoken to her that way. . .not ever.

Four

THE next Monday morning Jen's father skipped his morning jog. He said he needed to buy new shoes before he ran again. When he came to the breakfast table with several cuts on his face, he laughed, slightly embarrassed. "Ellie, I guess I'll have to break down and use that electric. . .thing"—he made a motion of shaving his jaw—"that your folks gave me." He touched one of the cuts and winced.

"Maybe you do need your eyes checked," her mother said. "Want me to make an appointment?"

"It's not my eyes. It was a faulty blade. Or have you and Jenny been using my razor to shave your legs?"

Jen tried to make a joke out of it. "No, Daddy, I only used it to peel potatoes."

He sprinkled wheat germ over his fruit and

yogurt. "I'm starved this morning." Suddenly he got up, crossed to the desk, and began fumbling through papers. "Ellen, did you see my notes on the Bagley case?"

"You never leave your work on the kitchen desk," Jen's mother said.

"What?" He stood staring down at the desk for a moment. "I know that!" he said sharply. "I thought you might have moved my papers."

"I didn't move them," her mother said. "I didn't see them."

"Maybe I left them at the office. I'm going now." He absently kissed Jen and her mother. "See you tonight."

"But you haven't eaten a bite," Jen's mother said. "It's only seven-thirty. You have plenty of time to get to work."

"I don't have time. I have a nine o'clock appointment. Anyway, I'm not hungry."

He had just said he was starved. Jen caught her mother's eye, and they both looked quickly away.

☆ ☆ ☆ ☆ ☆

Later that morning, Jen, Caroline, and their friend Mindy Wallace were in the pool, floating on rubber mattresses. The phone rang. Jen raised up. Suddenly she felt chilled, although the temperature was in the high eighties already.

Rosita, who was in the kitchen making tortillas, answered the phone. She came to the patio door. "Jen, it's your papa's office. An important client is waiting, and he hasn't come in to work yet. Maybe you should call your mama."

The chill deepened. Shivering now, Jen climbed out of the pool. She threw her towel around her shoulders and hurried to the kitchen. She glanced at the clock. It was ten-thirty. She turned to Rosita. "Daddy left before eight this morning." Her chest felt heavy. "Do you think he could have had an accident?"

"No, no. He probably ran out of gas or had car trouble. But call your mama."

A secretary answered the phone. "Tell my mother it's an emergency," Jen said so she wouldn't be put on hold for an hour.

When her mother came on the line, she sounded out of breath and worried. "Honey, what's wrong?"

"It's Dad. His office called and said he hasn't come in."

"Oh, I thought something terrible had happened."

"Mom, I'm scared."

"You're getting to be a regular worrywart. He's never had an accident in his life."

An accident wasn't the only thing that worried Jen. Her father had been acting oddly. Maybe he didn't love her and Mom anymore, she thought. Maybe he just took off like Caroline's dad. Or maybe he was sick again and was in the hospital. There was something wrong. A nameless, dark fear hovered over her, like a vaguely remembered nightmare.

"I'm sure everything's all right." Jen's mother reassured her. "I'll find out what's happened and call you back. He probably just ran out of gas."

"That's what Rosita said." Jen felt a little relieved. "I'll stay by the phone. Bye, Mom."

When Jen hung up, she turned to find Caroline and Mindy at the kitchen door. "Is your dad okay?" Caroline asked.

"I don't know, but I sure hope so."

"How would you girls like some cookies and milk?" Rosita asked. For Rosita, the answer to any problem was a plate of fresh cookies and a glass of cold milk.

"Hey, yeah, I'm starved," Caroline said. "We didn't have a thing in the house to eat this morning."

Rosita fixed a tray, and Jen took it into the family room so they could play records.

Mindy was looking at the rows and rows of records. "Wow, did your dad used to be a disk jockey, or what? I've never seen so many albums."

Mindy was little, red-haired, and a terrific ice skater. She'd been to Jen's house plenty of times, but never in this room.

"My dad loves music. He plays the guitar, the piano, and bass. He and mom have been collecting records for ages. Some are really old—seventy-eights." She switched on the stereo and put on a rock album. "This album's mine."

They all sat on the floor by the coffee table munching cookies to the beat of the song. But the cookies choked in Jen's throat. Her mind was on her father, not the music.

It was afternoon when Jen's mother finally called back. "I told you everything was all right," she said. "Your dad had a flat tire and couldn't find a telephone." Jen caught an odd tone to her mother's voice. "He said he'd try to get home early tonight."

Relief flooded over Jen. "I was so worried."

"I know, but it's all right now. Tell you what, ask Rosita if she'll fix some snack food. You three can invite some more of your friends over for a pool party."

"Oh, Mom, thanks. How many can I ask? Is it okay to invite some boys? Can we dance, too?"

"Eight is a good number. Yes, you can invite boys. And you can dance in the living room."

"Thanks, Mom. See you tonight."

Jen ran out to the patio. "Hey, guess what? My dad just had a flat tire, and he's okay. Mom says I can have a party, and we can invite some boys and dance in the living room. Who should we ask?"

Jen often had pool parties and barbecues, but she had never asked boys over to dance before. The rest of the afternoon, the three of them planned the party and chose the records. They invited one more girl, three boys from Valley Academy, and Gary Sivert. Everybody accepted—except Gary.

"I'd like to come over, Jennifer," Gary said, "but I have to take care of my granddad tonight."

"Sure. Maybe next time." As Jen hung up the receiver, she wondered if that had only been an excuse. What was he, a babysitter for old people? He probably just didn't want to hang out with seventh and eighth graders.

That afternoon, her father came home early. Jen hurried to greet him. "Daddy," she said, giving him a hug, "you sure had us worried."

He sank down on a lounge in the patio. "Worried? Just because I had a flat tire?"

Jen sat at the foot of the lounge. "Where were you, anyway? I didn't think you could go a half a mile without finding a phone."

He laughed, but there was an edge to his voice. "What is this, kitten, the third degree? Are you getting in practice to be a trial lawyer?"

She hung her head and stared at her hands. "No. It's just that you always tell me to call if I have trouble."

"Well, I couldn't find a phone! And when I did it was out of order. I don't know what's wrong with the phone company. They never repair their—their thingamabobs."

Jen flung her arms around his neck. "I'm just glad you're okay."

"Me, too" he said. "Now, let's go see what's cooking for dinner. I'm starved."

"That's because you didn't eat breakfast."

"Of course I ate breakfast. I always eat breakfast after my morning jog."

Jen looked at him, puzzled, but didn't argue. "Guess what? Mom said I could have a party. . .with boys. And we're going to dance."

"It sounds like fun. Did you invite that good-looking boy—what's his name—the tennis player?"

"Gary? I don't think he likes me. I asked him, but he has to take care of his grandfather. I mean, is that a dumb excuse, or is that a dumb excuse?"

"You never know. He seemed like a nice young man." Jennifer's dad looked at her for a long moment. "Parties, boys. . .my little girl is growing up too fast."

It wasn't fast enough, Jen thought. She wished she were grown up so she'd know what was going on. "Well, I have to get dressed and help with dinner. The kids will be here at seven."

☆ ☆ ☆ ☆ ☆

The party was slowly going down the tubes. Everybody they'd invited danced well, but all the boys were on one side of the room. The girls were standing on the other.

Finally, in desperation, Jen went to find her father.

"Daddy, what'll I do," she moaned. "Nobody's having any fun."

"You need an ice breaker," he said. "Go on back and turn off the music."

Jen hurried to the living room and switched off the stereo. "Hey, everybody, I have a surprise."

50

Her father came into the room carrying his guitar and walking like John Wayne. "Now listen up, pilgrims, and listen good." Then he went into his impersonation of John Wayne singing "Tiptoe Through the Tulips."

The kids laughed and clapped. "More! More!"

As many times as Jen had watched her father perform, she never grew tired of it. She bet nobody else in the world had a better father than she did. He did a few more impersonations and then said, "All right, it's dance time." He left, doing his Charlie Chaplin strut.

Then everyone began to dance. It was eleven before anybody realized it. Her father came in to break up the party. "Who needs a ride?" he asked.

No one did. Everyone was talking at once as they gathered up their things.

"It was a great party."

"That was the best cheese dip I ever ate."

"Do you need any help cleaning up?"

"No, I'll do it in the morning," Jen said.

"Mindy and I will come over and help," Caroline said. Then she whispered, "I think Rick likes me. We're playing miniature golf tomorrow night."

"He hardly danced with anybody but you.

51

I'd say he likes you," Jen whispered back.

Jen waved to everyone. "Good night. Thanks for coming."

She closed the door, smiled at her dad, and sighed happily. It had been a great party. Of course it would have been better if Gary had been there.

Her dad put his arm around her shoulder. "Mom's in the hot tub. Want to join us?"

"You bet. I'll get into my suit."

Jen loved the bedtime ritual of relaxing in the hot tub. She enjoyed listening to her parents talk about their jobs. But tonight, when she joined them, they abruptly stopped talking.

Nobody said anything for a bit, then her mother gave her a strained smile. "How did the party go?"

"Everybody seemed to enjoy it, at least after Dad got it going."

Her father leaned back with a groan. "I don't know when I've been so tired." He hesitated, but Jen knew by his tone that he was going to say something else. She had watched him in the courtroom, and he always seemed to stop and gather all his energy before he had anything important to say.

"Jenny, your mother was just telling me I've been rough on you. I guess I have been a bit irritable at times lately."

"Irritable?" her mother said with a smile. "A teased rattler is better tempered."

"I'm really sorry. It's just that I've been under a lot of stress lately. The Bagley case, and the new law clerk at the office. . .I wish our vacation started tomorrow instead of the middle of August."

"Me, too," Jen said. "Caroline and I can hardly wait to go out in the new boat and go water skiing. I hope I still remember how since last summer."

"I've been thinking," her father said. "Why don't we go on the Fourth of July? I can take Friday off, and Monday's a holiday."

"Oh, I can't," her mother said. "Craig finally looked at my script and said it needed rewriting. I'll have to work on it the whole weekend. But you two go. It would be good for both of you."

"Can Caroline come along? Please, Daddy?"

"Sure. Why not?"

"I'll get the camping gear ready in the morning," Jen said. "We'll need two tents, the skis and—"

"Not this time, honey. I'm too tired to wrestle with tents and the boat. I know a nice place in the mountains—you know, Ellen, where we went when we were first married.

Mountain Wilderness or Wildwood—oh, well, the name doesn't matter. We can get a cabin."

"You mean Idyllwild. But everything will be rented by now," her mother said. "One of my friends at work has a cabin on a lake at Pine Ridge. Maybe I could rent it."

"That sounds good to me. How about you, Jenny? We can swim and hike. There's a lot to do besides boating and water skiing."

"Sure, Daddy. It'll be fun." She was a bit disappointed, but just being with him was enough. "Can Caroline and I sleep in tents? We'll put them up and everything. I know how."

"I suppose so."

"And can we eat anything we want and stay up late and—"

"Don't push your luck, young lady," he said with a scowl. Then he grinned and hugged her. "We're going to have a great time."

Five

ON Thursday evening, Caroline's mother dropped her off at Jen's.

"Now, don't get sunburned. And stay out of the poison oak. Did you remember insect repellent? And see that you mind Mr. Burke."

"Yes, Mother," Caroline said with a pained voice.

"Did you put in warm pajamas? It's always cold in the mountains."

"Mom, I'm not a baby. Good-bye."

Jen grinned and helped Caroline bring in her things—a canvas suitcase, a backpack, a sleeping bag, and a large grocery sack.

"Mom thought I should furnish some of the food," Caroline said. "I have marshmallows, wieners, potato chips, and good stuff that your dad doesn't approve of."

The two of them helped pack the station wagon, which Jen's mother usually drove.

They needed the extra room for all their supplies. Rosita had packed enough food in two huge ice coolers to last them a month.

At eight-thirty, Jen's mother told Jen and Caroline to start getting ready for bed.

"But, Mom, it's hardly dark out yet," Jen complained.

"I want us to be on the road by five-thirty," Jen's dad said. "We'll eat breakfast on the way."

Jen and Caroline got ready for bed and laid out their clothes for morning. Jen pulled back the blue and white heirloom bedspread that Grandmother Nesbitt had given her. It was a nuisance to fold every night, but her grandmother would never forgive her if it got hurt.

"Jen, do you know if there'll be any kids our age at this place?"

"I don't think so. It's a private lake. Mom said the cabin's only partly built."

"Who cares about boys when we have your dad. He is one gorgeous hunk."

She said it like a joke, but Caroline wasn't the first of Jen's friends to have a crush on her dad. "Did you and Rick have a good time playing miniature golf?" Jen asked.

"He's a real jerk. All he wanted to talk about was playing video games. And he had to drag along his little brother. I get enough of ten-year-old boys when I visit my dad. I think boys should be put in a special box and frozen from the age of two to fourteen, then brought back to life."

Jen laughed. "I can just see a fourteen-year-old boy who comes out of a deep freeze and all he knows are three words—da-da, doggie, and bye-bye."

A knock on the door startled them. "You two girls quiet down in there," Jen's mother said. "Five o'clock will be here before you know it."

"We're practically asleep, Mom. Good night."

☆　☆　☆　☆　☆

At five-thirty sharp the station wagon pulled out of the driveway. The freeway was crowded with campers, vans, trailers, and motor homes. It always seemed to take forever to get out of the Los Angeles area, Jennifer thought.

Jen noticed that her dad was unusually quiet. She and Caroline played word games with roadside signs. After a couple of hours, they turned off the freeway and ate breakfast in a small town.

Back in the car, her father got out the road

map and directions. "Jenny, see if you can read your mother's note. Is that number a five or a two?"

"A five," Jen said, surprised because it was easy to make out. Mom was right, she thought. Dad does need glasses. No wonder he made a mistake on the income tax.

"Okay, it should take us another two or three hours depending on the roads."

They began to climb into the mountains. The scenery changed from dry hillsides to pines and juniper. The last few miles were over a dirt road that didn't look like it had been used since the rainy season. It was almost noon when they arrived at a small lake, surrounded by pines. The road ended in front of a clearing. The "cabin" was merely a foundation and some wall supports.

"It's a good thing you girls wanted to sleep in tents," Jen's father said.

"You can use one of ours. Caroline and I can share one."

Caroline gave Jen a dirty look. "I was hoping we'd sleep in a cabin. I don't know anything about tents. I've never camped out in my life except in Mrs. Nickelson's backyard when we were Brownies."

"Don't worry," Jen said. "It's fun."

They got out and stretched. Caroline was

looking around. "Isn't there a bathroom?"

Jen grinned at her father. "I think I'd better explain a few things to her," Jen said. "Come on, Caroline. The 'bathroom' is behind that tree over there."

They unloaded the car, pitched the two tents, and made sure the food was safe from the animals. They ate sandwiches and drank fruit punch. Her father picked up a crust that Caroline had left on the ground. "We don't want any midnight visitors." He looked around. "You girls want to go swimming or exploring first?"

"Aren't there any other people up here?" Caroline asked. "I thought there'd be boats and kids and stuff."

"There will be when we go to Big Bear," Jen said. "But this will be just as much fun."

Caroline looked doubtful, then she gave her usual good-humored grin. "Let's explore first." She looked around. "Wow, the sky is so blue. And listen." There wasn't a sound except a breeze whispering in the pines, a bird singing, and the soft buzz of bees. "It's so quiet—no traffic, no dogs, no airplanes."

After the haze and smog of the city, the air seemed so fresh with the scent of pines. Jen's father stretched his arms to the sky. "This is what I needed. Come on, girls, get your boots and backpacks on, and let's go. Don't forget your whistles. I want you to wear them at all times."

When they were ready, they followed a creek through the forest. Their footsteps hardly made a sound on the thick carpet of pine needles.

"Can't you almost imagine there's an Indian hiding behind that big tree?" Caroline asked in a hushed voice.

As they walked, Jen's father told them a story about an Indian girl who got lost in the forest. Jen smiled to herself. Caroline didn't realize he was giving her a painless lesson in how to survive in the wilderness.

Near a large pine they saw tracks of a good-sized bear and smaller prints following it.

"I think we'd better head back," Jen's father said. "We don't want to tangle with a mama bear and her cubs."

Back at camp, Jen's father said he was going to take a nap. The rest of the day, Caroline and Jen swam and sunned and tried to paddle the kayak they found behind the cabin foundation.

Before sunset, Jen's dad built a campfire in an open area. He roasted potatoes and corn on the cob to go with Rosita's fried chicken. "Guess we'd better eat the watermelon while there's still plenty of ice," he said.

Caroline finished eating and groaned. "I've never eaten this much in my life. I'm stuffed. Everything tasted so good."

"It always does when you're out in the fresh air," Jen said.

They sat around the fire for a while. But by dark, they were all tired and ready for bed.

When they were in their sleeping bags, Caroline whispered, "Do you think that bear will bother us?"

"Don't worry about it. My dad will know what to do. Are you sorry you came along?"

"No way. I don't even care that there aren't any boys. Jen, your dad is really neat."

Usually they would have talked for a long time, but they both fell asleep almost immediately.

The smell of frying bacon awakened them. They crawled out of their tent to find Jen's father fixing breakfast. Jen was surprised to see bacon, fried potatoes, and even coffee perking. Apparently he had given up yogurt and wheat germ...on this trip, anyhow.

Saturday and Sunday were filled with swimming, hiking, kayaking, fishing, and horseshoes, a game that Caroline had never heard of. On their last night, they sat around the campfire. Jen's father got his guitar from the car and played. Jen joined him in singing old cowboy songs, and crazy songs like "The Man On The Flying Trapeze." Caroline joined in on songs like "Row, Row, Row Your Boat" and "You Are My Sunshine."

He ended with "Yesterday, When I Was Young." It had been such a wonderful time. Impulsively, Jen leaned over and hugged her father. "Oh, Daddy, I love you. I'll never forget these few days. . . never."

☆ ☆ ☆ ☆ ☆

During the night a mountain storm blew in. Thunder awakened Jen and Caroline. Lightning zigzagged across the sky. Then moments later thunder crashed.

"It's a lot scarier up here than at home," Caroline whispered.

"There's nothing to be afraid—"

A flash filled the tent with light. Jen saw Caroline's frightened face. "Daddy," Jen called, "can we come in with you?"

"It's only a two-man tent, but come on," he said.

They grabbed their sleeping bags and crawled into his tent. Then the rain began and continued through the night. None of them got much sleep. At dawn it was still raining hard, and the wind was howling. "Sorry, kids, but I think we'd better head home before those dirt roads are impassable."

By the time they got the car loaded they were all soaked, tired, and irritable. They piled into the front seat.

"My hair's sopping wet," Caroline said. "I'm freezing."

"Me, too. But you have to expect things like that on a camping trip," Jen explained.

Jen's father started the engine. He was fumbling with the knobs on the dashboard and muttering to himself."

"What's wrong?" Jen asked.

"Nothing's wrong," he shouted. He hit the dashboard with his fist. Then, incredibly, he burst into tears.

"Daddy! What is it?"

He just sat there, hunched forward, crying softly.

Jen was too embarrassed to look at Caroline. She had never seen her father cry. She'd never seen any man cry before. She didn't know what she should do.

Her father leaned his head on the steering wheel. "Jenny...I..." he mumbled.

She tried to make out what he was saying. "I can't understand you."

He raised up and gave a long quivering

breath. "I . . . I don't know how to turn on the windshield wipers."

There wasn't a sound in the car as Jen reached over and turned on the switch. She couldn't look at her father. "Are you sure you can drive?" she asked, trying to keep her voice from shaking.

"Of course I can drive. I—I'm just not used to the station wagon." Her father wiped his damp face and gave a strained laugh. "Boy, did I get soaked out there. You kids had better get in back and put on some dry clothes."

Silently, Jen and Caroline climbed over the seats and into the back. As they were changing, Jen's dad began to sing, "Stormy weather, me and my gals together. . . ."

All the way home he was singing and laughing and doing imitations of Donald Duck and Popeye. But it all seemed forced to Jen.

She watched him out of the corners of her eyes. His face was flushed, and his eyes were too bright.

Oh, Daddy, what's wrong? What's wrong?

Six

THEY arrived home shortly after noon. When they dropped Caroline off at her house, she smiled brightly and talked too fast. "I had a great time, Mr. Burke. Thanks for inviting me." Before Jen could say anything, Caroline opened her front door. "I'll talk to you, Jen." And she was gone.

Jen walked dejectedly back to the car.

"Caroline's a nice girl," her father said as they drove off. "Guess that storm kind of put a damper on all of us." He grinned at her. "That's a pun. Damp—damper."

She forced a smile. "That's not even good enough to be a groaner."

She stared out the window, wishing her dad wouldn't try so hard. She couldn't sort out her feelings. She was embarrassed because of the way he had acted. She was angry with Caroline for being embarrassed, too. And she was angry with her father for making her feel this way.

When they pulled into the drive, Jen's mother came out to the car. "Well, you two are back early. What happened?"

"There was a storm," her dad said. "I was afraid we'd get stuck up there."

Her mother kissed them both. "I got lots of work done while you were gone, but I was envying you. I'll bet you had a wonderful time."

"It was great," Jen said, hoping her voice sounded enthusiastic. Her mother looked at her oddly.

"We sure did," her dad said. "After the long drive I'm kind of tired, though. Think I'll relax in the hot tub and take a shower before I unload the car."

As soon as he was out of the room, Jen's mother asked, "All right, honey, what happened? Did you and Caroline have a fight?"

Jen shook her head. "Oh, Mom, the trip didn't help Daddy at all. Something's wrong. Something's really, really wrong."

Jen told her mother about her dad not remembering how to turn on the windshield wipers. "It was awful." She closed her eyes, trying to shut out the memory. "He just sat there and cried."

"Honey, I know it must have upset you, but your father's under a great deal of pressure at work. He lost an important case last week."

"He's lost cases before, but he's never acted like that."

"He could still be run-down from that bout with pneumonia. I'll try to get him to see the doctor." She patted Jen's cheek. "Don't worry. He'll be his old self before you know it."

Jen pushed down the fears. Sure, she told herself, he had just been upset. Everybody gets upset sometimes. She wanted to phone Caroline and say, "Promise you won't tell anybody about it." But she couldn't bring herself to make the call. Anyway, Caroline was probably taking a nap. Or maybe she was busy. I'll call tomorrow, Jen thought.

But she didn't call the next day, nor the day after. The following afternoon, Caroline showed up at the back door. "Want to ride your bike with me to The Carnival and get a soda or something?"

"Sure. Wait for me." Jen got her money and yelled to Rosita. "I'm going to ride my bike to The Carnival with Caroline. We'll be back by four."

"Be careful," Rosita said, as she always did.

As Jen and Caroline rode to the restaurant, neither said anything for a bit. Caroline was the first to break the uncomfortable silence. "I've really been busy since we got back from the mountains."

"Me, too." Jen lied. "I had a million things to do."

They both pulled up and stopped. "I wasn't busy at all," Jen admitted. "I wanted to call you. . . ."

"I picked up the phone a dozen times." Caroline shrugged. "I just didn't know what to say."

"It's all right," Jen said. "I know how you felt."

"Is your dad okay?"

"He's fine. He's just under stress."

Jen was beginning to be sick of that word. Her father had refused to go to the doctor, saying, "You know how stressful my job is."

"I was afraid he was having a nervous breakdown or something," Caroline said, then tried to laugh. "I mean, you should have seen your face, Jen."

"I was embarrassed to have anybody see him cry that way."

"It wasn't as bad as that time you saw my dad come home drunk. Now, that was really embarrassing."

"Let's not talk about either of those times. Okay?"

"Sure. And look, Jen, don't worry. I won't tell anybody, not even my mom."

☆ ☆ ☆ ☆ ☆

A big weight seemed to have lifted from Jen. During the next few weeks her father was preoccupied and impatient sometimes. But he was never short with Jen, not even when he thought she had moved some of his notes. He cut down on his activities. He no longer jogged every morning. And he only swam twenty laps instead of forty.

After breakfast one Saturday, he seemed in an unusually good mood. He took Rosita's hand. "You my beautiful Rosita, are a genius in the kitchen. You could be a chef in the finest restaurant."

Rosita beamed happily as she cleared the table.

He moved about the room, rearranging papers on the desk, straightening the table mats, and humming tunelessly. "Ellie, I have a golf date with the old man this afternoon," he said, making a face.

He hated playing golf with his boss.

"How about the three of us going to the club now, playing some tennis, and eating lunch there?"

"I should do some work,'" her mother said, but not with much conviction.

"Come on, we haven't played tennis in weeks."

"I want to go," Jen said. This was Caroline's weekend to be with her father, and Mindy was on vacation at the beach.

"Sure, why not," her mother said. "I'm ahead of schedule on the script. And I could certainly use a break. What does Mr. Calvert want, anyway?"

Mr. Calvert was the senior partner in the law firm of Calvert, Whitworth, Danforth and Burke. Mr. Calvert had taken Jen's father into the firm right from law school and groomed him to be a partner. The families never saw each other socially, except at the yearly party at Mr. Calvert's Beverly Hills mansion.

"He's been nagging me about overworking . . . just like someone else I know."

Jen's mother smiled and kissed her husband.

"I do not nag. I just want you to take care of yourself."

He patted his stomach. "I'm in great shape. Come on. Let's go."

"Do you need me tonight, Senora Ellen?"

"No, I don't think so, Rosita. But next week I'd like you to send the guest room draperies to the cleaners. My parents are stopping here on their way back from Hawaii."

Jen's father turned. "You didn't tell me they were coming."

"Oh, honey, I did, too. Anyway, they always stop here on their way home."

He went over to the calendar and looked at it for a moment. "Where does the time go?" he muttered to himself.

"Oh, Rosita," her mother said, "tell Juan to put a new washer in the guest room shower."

Jen's father frowned. "Can't you and Rosita plan this visit some other time?"

Jen's dad was usually so patient. Now he was jangling his car keys. "If you two don't hurry, I'm going on alone," he said and headed for the door.

"Just let us change into tennis outfits," her mother said.

He groaned. "I'll wait for you in the car."

Jen and her mother rushed upstairs, changed, and hurried out to the car. And after all their rushing, when they got to the club, they had to wait for a court.

The morning was perfect—not too hot and no smog. They found seats by the pool and ordered cold drinks.

"Jennifer?"

Jen turned at the sound of her name and

saw Gary Sivert smiling at her. "Hi," he said. He was carrying his tennis racket.

Her face did its usual coloring act. "Hello," she said coolly. She turned to her parents. "Mom, you've never met Gary." She introduced them.

Jen's dad shook Gary's hand as if they'd never met before. "Nice to meet you."

Jen hoped Gary hadn't noticed. "Have you been playing?" Jen asked.

"No. I couldn't get a court."

"We have one reserved," her father said. "Why don't you join us? We can make it doubles, you and my wife against Jenny and me."

Gary sat down with them, and Jen's father ordered Gary a soda.

"How was your party, Jennifer?" Gary asked.

"We had a great time. You should have seen Dad do his impression of John Wayne."

"I'm really sorry I missed it," Gary said.

He sounds sincere, Jen thought. Maybe he was telling the truth, after all.

Nobody said anything for a bit. Usually Jen's father would have been telling funny stories, but today he was just staring at the water. When they finally got a court, he seemed uninterested in the game.

Jen loved to play partners with her father, but not today. He dove for balls and missed. He tried for an easy overhead shot and didn't come close to hitting the ball. He looked at his racket as if there were a hole in it, then laughed. "I guess I really do need glasses."

Gary and Jen's mother won the first set, six to two. Jen and her dad couldn't seem to get together. He would take balls that should have been hers. Then one would come right down the middle between them.

"Jenny, if you're not going to go for the ball, I might as well play by myself," he said, his voice edged with irritation.

"But, Daddy, I thought you—"

"David," her mother said, breaking in, "I'm dying of thirst. How about going inside for a tall, icy glass of tea?"

"I don't—"

Again she broke in. "Please, Dave. I'm feeling rather faint. I can't take the heat."

"But, Mom, I don't want to go in yet," Jen said.

"There's no need to. You and Gary go ahead and play until lunch. We'll eat at one o'clock in the patio restaurant. Gary, would you like to join us?" her mother asked.

"Thanks, Mrs. Burke, but I have to be home by one-thirty. If it's okay with Jennifer, though, I'd like to play a few more games."

Jen and Gary played a set, which he won, but it was close. "I'll get you next time," she said.

"It's a date."

She felt her face flush. Of course he didn't mean a real date. It was just a phrase. It didn't mean anything. Or did it?

He walked her back to the clubhouse patio. "Thanks for the game," he said. "I like your folks. They're fun. Mine are always too busy."

"I just wish you'd seen Dad at his best. He's never played so badly. We think it's his eyes."

"Sure. Everybody has off days. Hey, I'll call you as soon as I have a free morning. Bye, Jennifer."

She liked the way he said Jennifer. Hardly anybody called her that except teachers and her grandmother. Somehow it sounded nicer when he said it. Jen watched him stride down the path to the bike rack. Next to her father, Gary was about the best looking guy she knew. And he was one of the nicest, too. He seemed so much more mature than the boys in her class. She hurried to join her parents in the covered patio.

During lunch her mother went to another table to speak to a friend from work. Jen and her father were talking about the new boat.

"We'll have the christening when we go up to Big Bear. We're going to call it *The Jenny*."

"Oh, Daddy, a boat named after me. I love it!"

"Hi, Dave, how's it going?"

Jen and her father looked up to see a neighbor who had moved away a few months before.

Jen noticed her father's blank look and spoke up. "Hello, Mr. Frazier, nice to see you again."

"Hello, Mr. Frazier, nice to see you again," her father mimicked.

Mr. Frazier slapped her dad's shoulder and laughed. "Same old joker, aren't you? Has the old neighborhood gone to pot since we moved away?"

As the two talked, Jen stared at her father. How could he not recognize a former neighbor? A new worry hit her. Maybe he was going blind!

Mr. Frazier gave her father another slap on the back. "Call me sometime, and I'll beat you at handball."

Jen's mother returned, and they finished their meal.

"I'm going down to the locker room to change my shoes," Jen's dad said. "Ellen, do you want to stay until after my golf game?"

"No, I need to get on home. Give me a call when you're through, and I'll come get you. Jen, you can stay and swim or play tennis if you want."

"No, I guess I'll go home, too."

"Okay, see you two later," he said. "Wish me luck that I don't accidentally beat the old man. He can't stand to lose."

As soon as he was out of hearing range, Jen said, "Mom, he didn't even know Mr. Frazier. They jogged every morning for seven years. How could he not know him?"

"Don't worry about it."

Jen felt frustrated. Nobody ever tells me anything, she thought. You'd think I was a baby or something.

Jen and her mother had only been home for an hour when her dad called. Jen answered the phone. Her dad sounded angry. "Pick me up right away. I'll be out by the pool. And hurry."

Jen and her mother got back into the car. "I feel like a cabdriver," her mother said.

A few minutes later they pulled into the parking lot. Jen started to get out when she saw Mr. Calvert heading toward them. "He sure looks mad," she whispered to her mother.

Mr. Calvert came right up to the car. "Ellen, I want to have a talk with you," he said without even saying hello.

"Right now? I came to pick up David."

"I know that. I don't want him to see us together. He has an appointment with a client Monday evening. If it's all right with you, I'll stop by your place about seven-thirty."

Jen's mother's face looked as perplexed as her voice sounded. "Uh—well—that's fine. But what's it about?"

Mr. Calvert glanced at Jen. "It's confidential." He turned on his heel like a soldier and headed back to the clubhouse.

Jen's mother let out a sigh. "Your father must have had a run-in with Mr. Calvert. You'd better go get—" She stopped as they saw Jen's father coming toward them. She opened the door and moved into the middle.

Jen's dad climbed into the driver's seat. "What was that old coot talking to you about?" he demanded.

Jen's mother never lied, but now she said, "He wanted me to call his wife about helping out in some charity benefit."

"Oh." He accidentally put the car into reverse and nearly smashed into the car behind them. "That man really burns me sometimes," he said. "I think I'll do what I've always wanted to do—open my own law office. Who needs him?"

The tires squealed as he took a corner too fast. "Dave, you're too upset to drive. Let me take the wheel."

"What's the matter? You think I'll get lost!"

"I don't know what you're talking about. You're driving too fast. Slow down."

Much to Jen's relief, her father did slow down. He turned to grin at both of them. "Well, if I do get a ticket, I know a good lawyer."

Seven

JUST before seven-thirty on Monday evening, Jen headed upstairs to wash her hair. "Call me as soon as Mr. Calvert leaves," she said to her mother.

Although she had been expecting the sound, the door chimes startled her. She knew she should go on up the stairs, but this meeting concerned her father. Don't I have a right to know what's going on? she wondered.

She sat on a step just above where the stairs curved. She couldn't see the living room from there, but no one could see her either.

Mr. Calvert came in. Her mother offered him a cold drink. "No, thank you, Ellen. I want to get this unpleasant business over with. Are we alone?"

"Yes. What is it you want to talk to me about, Mr. Calvert?"

"I don't know quite where to start. I may as

79

well be blunt. Is David drinking these days?" Mr. Calvert asked.

Jen could almost hear the relief in her mother's voice as she answered, "Good heavens, no!"

"I know this is personal, but are you two having marital problems?"

"No. No more than any couple. Mr. Calvert, what are you getting at? Why these questions?"

"Because there's something seriously wrong with David. I've been trying to get him to see a psychologist friend of mine, but he just gets angry."

"Well, I don't blame him. Why should he see a psychologist?"

There was a long pause. Jen wanted to peer around the corner to see what was happening. Then Mr. Calvert answered. "Ellen, surely you've seen the change in him recently. He's irresponsible and impatient. He loses track of time and insults his clients. His work is suffering."

"He's been upset over losing that big insurance fraud case."

"He lost it because of incompetence."

"How can you say that? He's the best attorney in the firm!"

"He was, Ellen. He's not any more. As of

next week, I'm ordering him to take a leave of absence."

Jen could picture the stunned look on her mother's face. "How—how long?" her mother asked.

"That's up to him. I strongly suggest you get him to a doctor. I know this seems harsh and uncaring to you, but I have no choice. He's like a son to me. And like most sons who won't listen to their fathers, he won't listen to me. You have to do something, Ellen."

There was another long pause, then Jen heard Mr. Calvert's heavy footsteps on the hardwood floors. She sat there feeling numb, disbelieving. A psychologist? Does Mr. Calvert think Daddy is crazy? She started downstairs when she heard her mother on the phone.

"Mother, it's me, Ellen . . . Yes, I know it's nearly eleven o'clock back there . . . I want to ask a favor . . . Can you change your plans and stop over here on your way to Hawaii? . . . Because I need your advice . . . Yes . . . Will you do it? . . . I'll pick you up at the LA airport . . . Friday evening at six . . . I'll tell you all about it when you get here . . . All right . . . Thanks, Mother. I love you, too. Bye."

Jen started slowly down the stairs, then heard soft crying. She looked around the curve and saw her mother sink down on the couch and bury her face in her hands. "Oh, David," she whispered, "what's happening to us?"

Jen felt tears sting her own eyes. She crept silently back upstairs.

☆　☆　☆　☆　☆

On Friday, Jen's father came home early. He tossed his briefcase across the room and laughed exuberantly. "Jenny, I have good news. I've decided not to wait until the middle of August for a vacation. I'm starting it right now." He picked her up and swung her around. "We can swim and jog and play tennis every day."

Jen swallowed the huge lump in her throat. She wanted to cry for him. He was trying so hard to pretend the leave of absence was all his idea. She managed to get her voice under control. "That's great."

He went to the freezer and took out a carton of ice cream. "Let's celebrate with a triple decker banana and nut and chocolate syrup sundae."

Rosita came in from the dining room. "Oh, no you don't, Senor David. I am fixing a fancy meal for Grandmama and Grandpapa Nesbitt. We're having leg of lamb and asparagus and—"

"Stop! We'll behave. We just want one little

spoonful?" he begged like a small boy.

Rosita pretended to scowl. "One spoonful each. No more."

While they slowly licked the ice cream, Jen noticed his shoulders slump for a moment. Then with an obvious effort, he smiled. "It's going to be great to have more time for the things I've always wanted to do. I can read more and learn to play the tenor sax. And I can do crossword puzzles. Do you know, I've never had time to finish one?" He slammed the spoon into the sink. "I hate crossword puzzles!"

"Daddy," Jen said quietly, "we'd better get ready. Mom, Grandpa, and Grandma will be here any minute."

"If they don't come soon," Rosita moaned, "my beautiful roast will be ruined."

Jen's mom and grandparents arrived more than an hour late. As they came in the front door, Jen ran to greet them. "Hi, Grandma. Grandpa."

Her grandmother was slim and pretty in her white dress. Her grandfather was wearing walking shorts and a brilliantly flowered Hawaiian shirt, much to Grandma's obvious disgust.

As always her grandmother offered her cheek. She never kissed anybody. Jen's mother said it was because New Englanders were aloof. Her grandfather hugged her. "I swear you've grown a foot since we saw you. Is your dad feeding you Miracle Grow?" He shook hands with her father. "David. Good to see you."

"Katherine. Charlie. You two picked a good time to stop over," Jen's father said. Jen saw her grandmother wince at the name Charlie. "I just started my vacation today," her dad added.

Jen's mother turned quickly and gave her husband a look of surprise, which she tried to cover. "That's wonderful, Dave," she said. "I'm glad you finally decided to take a rest."

Jen looked at her grandparents, trying to tell if her mother had said anything to them about her father. She decided they didn't know yet.

At dinner, Jen couldn't enjoy the wonderful meal. She kept worrying that her dad would do or say something embarrassing. But he was charming and full of funny stories. And after dinner, they all sat out by the pool in the balmy night air. Her dad played his guitar and sang. And even Jen's grandmother relaxed enough to sing.

After a while, Jen's mother said, "Dave, why don't you and dad go into the hot tub. You too, Jen. Mother and I want to gossip about home."

"I know what you want to talk to Grandma about," Jen whispered. "Can I come with you?"

Her mother hesitated. "I suppose so."

Jen's grandmother looked from one to the other. "Ellen, what's going on?"

"Mother, the problem is that I don't know what's going on. David hasn't been himself for weeks, even longer, I think."

"What do you mean, not himself. He hasn't changed a bit. I must say, if anyone's changed, it's you and Jennifer. You're both tense. Jennifer just picked at her food."

"That's because we're worried about Dave."

"Well, I can't understand why. He looks marvelous. Is that the problem? Aren't you two getting along? My dear, every marriage goes through periods of adjustment. How old is David now?"

"He'll be forty-three this September. But what's his age got to do with anything?"

"When men start to feel their age, they do strange things. Why, I remember the day your father turned forty, he went out and bought an exercise machine and a whole new wardrobe."

"Mother, this is serious."

"Sometimes it can be. What you need is a marriage counselor or your family minister."

Jen's mother bit her lip and looked away.

"But, Grandma," Jen began. "Dad's been acting—"

"Never mind, honey," her mother said. "She's right. I'll talk to our minister."

Jen started to argue, but her mother gave her a stern look.

Jen's heart sank. Isn't mother ever going to admit that something is terribly, terribly wrong?

☆ ☆ ☆ ☆ ☆

The enforced vacation seemed to help Jen's father, at least for a while. Jen and her dad swam and played tennis. Sometimes Caroline, Mindy, and even Gary joined them.

The summer days sped by, and it was almost time to go to Big Bear. Everything was wonderful until the evening her mother came home with her good news. "Dave! Jen! Rosita!"

They all came running to the kitchen. "It's finally going to happen. Craig's decided to do my *Death Is No Angel.* We start production next week. I can't really believe it yet."

"Mom, that's super," Jen said.

"Honey, I told you you'd be famous. I'll bet you win an Emmy award."

Dinner was a regular celebration. "Rosita," her father said, "you are going to be a guest. I am going to fix dinner."

Rosita glanced at the spaghetti sauce cooking. "But Senor David, dinner is all—"

"No argument. The three of you go soak in the hot tub while I whip up my delectable, Indian specialty."

"Oh, Dave, not chicken curry."

"Yes, *Murgi Kari* and saffron rice. Rosita, we do have chicken in the freezer?" She nodded.

Jen's dad started looking through the spices on the rack. He took out several jars. "We'd better have some saffron. Jenny, did you know it takes more than 75,000 crocus blossoms to make one pound of saffron?"

"No, but that's a lot of croaked crocuses," she answered, and everybody groaned.

"Get out of here, and leave the master chef to his gastronomic masterpiece." He was banging through cupboards and drawers. "Now, who's taken the—you know—that drainer thing."

"You mean the colander?" Rosita asked. "It's in the cupboard under the stove."

"Why don't you keep it in the same place? This kitchen's a mess!"

"Senor David, that colander has been in the

same cupboard since you moved in."

Jen's mother gave her husband a long look. "Are you sure you want to fix this meal?"

"Of course I do. Now, leave me alone."

Rosita shrugged and turned off the heat under the sauce.

Jen, Rosita, and her mother were just getting into the spa when her father came rushing out. "Rosita? Don't we have any ginger root?"

"I don't think so, Senor David."

"Every well stocked kitchen should have ginger root! How can I make this dish without it? You deliberately didn't buy it so I couldn't make my specialty."

"Dave, you're being unreasonable," Jen's mother said.

"Stay out of this, Ellen. You never did know how to treat servants."

Jen gasped. Rosita and Juan had never been servants.

"Rosita, you just don't want anybody in the kitchen. Isn't that right? Well, I'm sick of tacos and enchiladas, and I'll choke if I eat another tortilla." He spun around and headed back to the kitchen.

"Rosita, he didn't mean that," Jen's mother said. "You know he thinks of you and Juan as family."

"I think I should go home now."

"No, please stay. These flashes of anger only last for a while. He—"

A yell from the kitchen cut her off. They ran inside to find her father at the stove shaking his hand in the air. Hot grease was spattering everywhere.

"Rosita, where did you hide the potholders! I've burned myself, and it's your fault. You're fired. Get your things and get out!"

"David, are you crazy?" her mother asked. "Rosita, you're not going anywhere."

Rosita just looked at him for a moment. Then she handed him a potholder from its spot by the stove, turned on her heel, and left the room.

Jen's father was frantically turning the knobs on all the burners. The rice was boiling all over the stove. And the chicken was burning, filling the air with greasy black smoke. "Will somebody turn off this blasted stove?" he yelled.

Jen's mother quickly turned off the stove and placed a lid over the frying pan. "It's off," she said coldly.

Jen's father's face seemed to crumple, and he sank to the floor. He pulled his knees up to his chest and began to cry softly, the way he'd done when he couldn't remember how to turn on the windshield wipers.

Jen's mother hurried over to him just as Rosita came in to the kitchen. Her eyes were red. Her voice was stiff as if she were trying not to cry. "Senor Burke, I am going now. Do you want Juan to stay on—"

Then Jen's mother stepped aside, and Rosita saw him on the floor crying. Her hand flew to her mouth and smothered her little moan. "Dear Mother of Jesus, help him. Help him, please."

☆　☆　☆　☆　☆

"David, I've made an appointment for you with Dr. Palmquist. I'm taking the day off."

Jen expected him to refuse, but all he said was, "You don't waste any time, do you?"

"May I go, too?" Jen asked.

"If you want to sit in a waiting room, I suppose it's all right."

Jen had to sit for two hours in the waiting room. When her parents came out, they would only say that her father had to go to a diagnostic center for a series of tests that would take four days.

Jen's mother couldn't take the time off for the first three days of tests, so Jen was allowed to go with her father. Again, it was waiting in corridors watching sick people shuffle past. Her dad had a neurological examination, a psychiatric evaluation, blood tests, tests that recorded brain activity, and tests that took pictures of the brain.

On the fourth day Jen's mother came along. It was the day they would find out what was wrong with her father. Jen was afraid to find out the truth and afraid not to. She sat in the waiting room while the doctors gave their evaluation.

When her parents finally came out, Jen searched their faces. Her mother was pale. Her father's face was unreadable.

"Daddy? What did the doctor say?"

He took a deep breath, then let it out in a quick gust. "Well, it's not—"

"They don't know what's wrong!" her mother said angrily. "All those tests and they still don't know for sure what's wrong. I'm making an appointment at the medical center. We're not going to take just one doctor's opinion."

"Ellie, I don't know if I can go through all the tests again."

"You have to, David. If not for me or for yourself, then do it for Jen. I just don't believe them."

He sighed. "I'm too tired to argue. If it will

make you accept the inevitable, then it's worth it, I guess."

Jen's heart sank. It must be something terrible. But maybe Mom's right, she thought. Maybe the doctors here didn't know what they were doing.

During the next week, her father went through the same tests and procedures while Jen waited. On the last day, she was sitting in the waiting room while her parents went in for the consultation. *Please let him be all right. Please let him be all right,* she thought over and over again.

The door opened, and her father stood there. "Jenny, I want you to be in here, too."

"David, no! She's too young."

"She's more mature than we are sometimes. Anyway, she has to know. You two are going to have to face this thing together."

Stiff-legged, wanting to run away, Jennifer walked slowly over to her father. He put his arm around her. "You've got to be strong, Jenny."

Her mother took one hand, her father, the other, and they walked into the doctor's office. The pneumatic door closed with a swoosh behind them.

Eight

A S Jen took a seat between her father and mother, her chest felt so tight she could hardly breathe. Her ears were ringing, and she didn't hear the first few things the doctor said.

"Jenny?" Her father touched her arm. "Jenny, honey, I know this is rough on you. But it's important that you hear what the doctor has to say."

Jen nodded her head.

"Okay, Doctor, let's have it. What's the verdict?" he asked.

"We've ruled out all the diseases we possibly can. All the tests were negative. So that leaves us with the diagnosis of Alzheimer's Disease."

"No! I don't care how many tests he's had, I still don't believe it," Jen's mother cried. "He's too young. Old people get Alzheimer's Disease."

"That's usually the case, Mrs. Burke. But I've had other patients in their forties and early fifties. Alzheimer's and old age don't necessarily go together. Changes occur in nerve cells in the brain that cause progressive intellectual deterioration."

Jen's father took a deep breath and let it out slowly. "So what happens next?"

"David, I don't want to hear any of this," Jen's mother said.

"Doctor, you must make her aware of what's going on." He got up slowly and walked to the far end of the room. He stood staring out the window.

"Mrs. Burke, the progress of the disease is different for each person. It's usually a slow, gradual decline. You may not notice much change, then one day he'll have more difficulty in finding the right word. He'll experience greater disorientation. His memory loss will become more pronounced, and there will be changes in personality, mood, and behavior. His judgment and concentration will become increasingly impaired. Speech and coordination will be affected. At some point he will be unable to dress himself and will become totally dependent on—"

"Stop it!" her mother cried and put her hands over her ears.

Jen's father came back to his chair. "Ellen, the first diagnosis was exactly the same, but you wouldn't listen. I asked the doctor to be blunt so you'd try to understand. Tomorrow, I may not even remember what he told us. You and Jenny have to know what's ahead."

"Mrs. Burke, I understand how difficult this is," the doctor said gently. "Your family doctor will put you in touch with social workers and occupational therapists. A geriatric nurse practitioner will come out to help you. She'll give you a list of books to read. And there are support groups, families who have been through it, who can help you deal with all the problems."

"But why him? Why should it strike a man in such good physical condition?" her mother asked.

"We don't know the cause."

For the first time, Jen spoke up. "Is—is it catching?"

"There's no evidence of that. There might be an inherited tendency to be vulnerable to the disease, but there's so much we don't know about it yet. At the present time, there's no cure."

Jen's father reached for her hand and squeezed it tightly. She bit her lip, trying not to cry, trying to be brave for him. *No cure . . .*

no cure . . . no cure. . . .

In a daze, she walked slowly out of the hospital to the parking lot. *No cure . . .* She closed her eyes against the piercing sun. An ambulance siren moaned. The hot afternoon wind rattled the fronds of the palms along the street. *No cure . . .* As she climbed into the backseat, hot air blasted her face. The leather seat burned. *No cure. . . .*

"David, I'll drive," her mother said. "You must be exhausted."

On the drive home, no one said anything for a while. Jen's father was the first to speak. "Ellen, I'm going to ask John to come to the house tomorrow night to help us make all the financial and legal arrangements."

"Dear heaven, can't it wait!"

"No," he said quietly. "It can't. I'll have to retire, and it's going to be a real financial burden. The doctor said my condition will only get worse. I know that eventually I'll have to go into a nursing home."

"No! Never!"

"Ellie, don't make this any harder for me. I want to provide for you and Jenny while I'm able."

He stared out the window for a bit, then he spoke slowly, "I've known something was wrong for quite a while. It's hard to explain."

He turned sideways in the seat so he was looking at both of them. "It's kind of like—like an eclipse of the moon. My mind is the moon, and the darkness is slowly blotting out the light."

Jen fought back the tears. How awful for him to know what's happening to his mind. It isn't fair! It isn't fair!

☆　☆　☆　☆　☆

The next night after Mr. Calvert left, Jen's mother told her some of the arrangements. "Our insurance doesn't cover custodial care, and your father's too young for Medicare. He's going to make out a living trust, so I can handle all the business affairs later on. We're going to have to sell the boat and cut down wherever we can. Mr. Calvert suggested we sell the house and buy a smaller one. I balked at that. Whatever happens, we're not going to let this thing totally change our lives."

But it did change Jen's life. She didn't have much time for Caroline and her other friends. Gary phoned several times to see if she wanted to play tennis, but she made excuses to everyone. She wanted to be with her father all the time now. They played tennis and jogged and swam and played games. But she could tell that some things, like Scrabble and trivia games, were becoming more and more difficult for him.

They decided to take the trip to Big Bear. And even though they didn't have the boat, Jen and Caroline had fun. The rest of the summer sped by, and then it was almost time to start school again. Jen was looking forward to being an eighth-grader.

One day, she and her mother were looking through Jen's closet. "You'll have to get some new clothes," her mother said. "You've grown a couple of inches over the summer."

"I can't even get into any of my shoes. But with Daddy not working, can we afford to buy anything?"

"I'll earn quite a bit from my play. If it's a success, maybe more of my scripts will be produced. We'll be all right."

And everything did seem to be all right. Jen's father was adjusting to his retirement. All those terrible things the doctor had talked about weren't going to happen to her father. He was too healthy, too strong, too young.

A few weeks after school began was the open house for parents to meet the teachers. Jen always looked forward to it, because she was so proud of her parents. This year, Jen wanted to brag to the drama coach about her mom having a play on TV. She was disappointed when her mother said she had to work late.

Jen's favorite class was music, and her favorite teacher was Mrs. Helmer. She dragged her father to the music room first. Earlier that day, Jen, Caroline, and a couple of other kids from the class had helped Mrs. Helmer set up a refreshment table. Rosita had furnished some of the cookies. Jen waved to her friends, but the teacher had given them orders not to congregate in little groups.

Jen was standing by her father, looking around at the other parents. Some of the men were younger than her father, but none of them were more handsome. No matter where he went, eyes followed him. Usually he would be talking to the other fathers. But tonight he didn't seem to be paying attention to anyone around them.

"Come on, Daddy," Jen said. "I want you to meet my music teacher." When he didn't respond, she tugged at his arm. "Daddy, come on."

"What?" He looked around as if surprised to find himself there.

"Mrs. Helmer's all by herself right now. Let's go talk to her."

Jen drew her father over to where her

teacher was standing. "Mrs. Helmer, I want you to meet my father, David Burke. Daddy, this is my music teacher."

"I'm happy to meet you. Mrs.—uh—yes, glad to . . ."

"I'm sorry my mother couldn't be here," Jen said quickly. "She's working tonight."

"I'm sorry, too. I understand she's an alumnus of Valley Academy. The drama class is especially looking forward to watching her play on tele—"

"Music teacher? I'm thinking of taking up the saxophone . . . or maybe drums."

"That's very nice," Mrs. Helmer said. "I can see where Jennifer gets her—"

Her father turned abruptly away, leaving the teacher standing there in mid-sentence. Before Jen realized what he was going to do, he walked over to the refreshment table. He picked up some cookies and began to juggle them.

Some of her friends, especially the boys who'd come to her party, were nudging each other. Jen knew they were expecting him to go into one of his comic acts.

Only it was soon obvious that this was no act. Her father was determinedly juggling the cookies, throwing them higher and higher. Jen was rooted to the floor, unable to move.

"Mr. Burke!" the teacher cried out.

As she started toward him, everybody turned to look just as one of the cookies fell into a pitcher of punch. He let the others drop to the floor. Then he stuck his arm into the pitcher and fished around, splashing punch all over himself.

"Got it!" he yelled gleefully and held up the disintegrating cookie. His sleeve was dripping red punch all over the white tablecloth.

The kids were snickering, and the adults were whispering. Their faces were a mixture of amusement and disgust.

Jen, sick with embarrassment, ran to her father, grabbed him by the arm, and pulled him to the door.

"Jen?" Caroline called. "Wait!"

"Daddy, come on!"

"Jenny, what's wrong?" he asked. "The open house isn't over."

Even out in the hall, Jen could still hear the laughter. They were laughing at her father. They were laughing at her. She hated them. She never wanted to face anybody again.

Nine

ALL night long, Jen's dreams were filled with faceless people laughing and snickering and pointing their fingers. The next morning all she wanted to do was stay in her room and never come out again. But a crash from the kitchen brought her out of bed. She met her mother in the hall, and they both raced downstairs.

They found her father on the floor. The rocking chair was on its side. The chair had apparently knocked over an end table and lamp.

"David, are you hurt?" They hurried to help him up.

"He must have been rocking too hard," Jen whispered, remembering the times she had tipped over backwards when she was little.

"Don't whisper behind my back!" he said. He got to his feet and looked around as if surprised to see the chair and table lying on their sides. Then he frowned. "Ellen, why haven't you fixed my dinner? I always have to wait for my dinner."

"It's breakfast time, not dinner time. What would you like? Some yogurt and fruit?"

"I hate yogurt. I'm going to soak in the hot tub."

As soon as he left the kitchen, Jen said, "Mom, I need to talk to you. You weren't home yet when Dad and I got back from school."

"What happened?"

"It was awful." Jen felt her face burn again as she told her mother how her father had acted. "Everybody laughed. I never want to go back to school."

"Honey, I know it's difficult, but you can't change schools now."

"The Academy costs a lot."

"I told you not to worry about money."

Before Jen could think of any more arguments, the phone rang, and her mother answered. "Oh, hello, Caroline."

Jen shook her head and mouthed the words, I don't want to talk to her.

"I'm sorry, dear, but Jen can't come to the phone right now. I'll tell her you called," she said and hung up. "Jen, don't do that again.

I won't lie for you."

"I don't want to talk to anybody. . .not ever again."

"Just be strong a little while longer. Your father's had a setback. But I'm sure in a month or so he'll be much better." Her mother turned, and Jen saw her helpless look.

The phone rang again. It was Mrs. Helmer, Jen's music teacher. "Jennifer, I just wanted to find out if everything's all right. You left in such a hurry. . . ." Her voice trailed off as if she didn't know what to say.

"Everything's just fine, Mrs. Helmer," she said stiffly. "I'm sorry but I have to go now. Thanks for calling. Everything's fine." As she hung up she noticed her hands were trembling. "Mom, I can't talk to anybody else."

"I'll buy an answering machine so we can screen the calls. I'm afraid your father doesn't pass on some of the messages." She tapped her head. "I'm getting as bad as he is. I forgot to tell you that a geriatric nurse practitioner is coming over right after school Monday. She's been wanting to come out. I couldn't put her off any longer. Be sure to come right home."

"Okay." Jen went out back to see if her father was all right. They worried about him turning the temperature of the hot tub too high. He was just sitting in the spa, staring into space and humming. Jen watched him for a minute. He seemed different somehow. It was as if a part of him were gone. Then he turned around and smiled, and he was her father again.

"Good morning, Jenny," he said as if this were the first time he'd seen her today. "I thought you and Mom were going to sleep until noon."

"I was kind of tired," she said.

"Well, you get some rest. Tonight we go to your school. I'm looking forward to meeting—"

Before Jen could tell him that the open house had been last night, Caroline came through the gate.

"Jen? Can I talk to you for a jiff?"

"Hello there, Caroline," he said. "Where have you been keeping yourself? Haven't seen you in weeks."

"But last night—"

"She's been busy," Jen broke in. "Come on up to my room," she said to Caroline. "See you later, Daddy."

In her room, Jen plunked down on the unmade bed. Caroline stood in the doorway for a moment, then walked slowly over to the bed and sat down. "I just wanted to tell your dad that I was sorry about what happened at school," Caroline said.

"It's okay. He doesn't remember what happened," Jen said with a sigh.

"Jen, I wish you'd tell me what's really wrong with him."

"I told you before. He had all those tests, but the doctors don't know for sure." That was only partially true. She couldn't bring herself to say he had Alzheimer's Disease. Alzheimer's was incurable. If there was no name for what was wrong with him, then maybe he'd get better.

"I'm really sorry, Jen."

Jen shrugged. "Thanks."

They sat in uncomfortable silence for a while. "What are you going to wear to Mindy's skating party tomorrow after school?" Caroline asked finally.

"I'm not going. Some nurse is coming over. I have to be here."

"Yeah?" Caroline said doubtfully. "Is it because you don't want to face the kids?"

That was true, too. "No, I really have to be here," Jen said. "Look, Caroline. Thanks for coming over, but I should help Mom. See you at school."

The next morning Jen managed to avoid most of her friends. After school she hurried home and found the nurse talking to her mother and Rosita in the living room.

"Jen, dear, this is Barbara Martin. My daughter, Jennifer."

"Hi," Jen said and perched on the arm of the sofa. She looked around. "Where's Daddy?"

"I asked Juan to keep him busy in the yard so Miss Martin can talk to us privately. I think it's a waste of time, but Miss Martin has been looking over the house and yard to see if it's safe." She turned to the nurse. "So, what do you think?"

"We'll get to that in a minute. First, I'd like to know if your doctor prescribed any medication?"

"No, nothing but some vitamins."

The nurse nodded. "Now, about the house and yard. It's not safe for your husband. And it's going to be extremely difficult for you to care for him here, especially as his condition worsens."

Jen's mother's smile was stiff. "But that will be years and years from now. The doctor said it was a slowly progressing disease. And my husband is a strong man, physically and mentally."

"Well, whenever it happens, you need to be prepared." The nurse smiled at Jennifer. "Why don't you point out some of the dangers.

See how many you can come up with."

Jen looked around. "I guess Dad could slip on these little rugs. The other day he knocked over a rocker and lamp. He could break a lot of Mom's antiques."

The nurse nodded. "You're right about the polished floors. They are dangerous. Anything else?"

"He burned himself trying to cook. The stove's dangerous. Oh, and there's the pool. Mom, do you think he could fall into the pool?"

"He's an excellent swimmer," her mother answered.

"Your father may retain some skills for a long time," the nurse said. "Other skills he could lose tomorrow. Later on, the pool and hot tub could both be dangerous."

"What about the car?" Jen asked, thinking about how he couldn't find the windshield wipers. Next time, it might be the brakes.

"Sooner or later you will have to stop him from driving," the nurse said.

"David will never agree to that."

"For men that's one of the most difficult things to give up."

"One good thing," Jen said, trying to change the subject before her mother got angry, "Daddy doesn't smoke. But we do have matches around for the grill and fireplaces."

"Good," Miss Martin said. "From now on, that's the way you have to think. Is there anything else?"

"Well, there are poisons for bugs in the garage . . . and all Dad's electric tools."

"And there's the electric carving knife," Rosita put in, "and my cleaning supplies."

"Wow," Jen said. "There must be lots of dangerous stuff around, like the medicines in the bathroom."

"It sounds like when Jen was a baby. I had to kid-proof everything."

"Precisely. Only please don't forget that Mr. Burke isn't a child."

"No one knows that better than I do, Miss Martin," Jen's mother said. "I'm sorry. I don't mean to be rude, but my nerves are about to snap." She sighed.

"I know how hard this is for you. Believe me, most people react the same way. I just have a few hints that might be helpful.

"Try to remember that when he's tired, ill, in pain, or hurried, he'll get more agitated and confused. A regular routine will make him feel more secure. Encourage him to do as much as possible for himself. And recreation is very important. I understand he enjoys music and sports. By all means, try to see that he maintains those interests."

"Oh, I can do that," Jen said. "As soon as I get home from school every day we can swim and stuff."

"Try not to let it bother you if he gets stubborn," the nurse continued. "Patients often resent the care-giver. Don't argue. Just stay calm."

The nurse gave other hints about gradually changing his clothing to more simple things— slip on shoes, pullover shirts instead of ones with buttons, socks of one color. She told Jen how to make labels for drawers and cupboards. "As he grows more and more confused, anything you can do to make life simpler for him, will make it easier for you.

"And one last thing. An ID bracelet would be helpful, one that says, 'Memory Impaired.' Now, any questions?"

Jen stared at her hands and mumbled, "What do I do when people make fun of Dad and laugh at him as if he were crazy?"

"I know that's a hard one to deal with. It's because people don't understand about Alzheimer's Disease. Just put it down to ignorance. One thing that might help though is a family support group. It helps to talk to other people with the same problems. I'll give you the name and phone number. They meet once or twice a month."

"I'm not interested in hearing a lot of tearful testimonials," Jen's mother said.

"It's not like that at all. The people in the group only want to help each other. I talk to different groups, and I must say I've never met more dedicated, courageous people in my life. Jennifer, you might be interested in next month's meeting. They are inviting young people. Most of them are grandchildren of patients with Alzheimer's. I think you'd find it very helpful. It's the second week in October." She jotted something on a paper and handed it to Jen. "Here's the time and place."

Jen shrugged. She wasn't sure she liked the idea of talking about her dad to a bunch of other kids. "I'll think about it."

Jen's mother thanked Miss Martin and showed her to the door. "I appreciate all your help, but I don't think my husband will ever get that bad."

"That's right," Jen said. "I'll help him. You'll see. He'll be back to work next month."

☆　☆　☆　☆　☆

But Jen's father didn't get any better. Instead, he grew rapidly worse. Jen's mother called Doctor Palmquist. "All you doctors told me Alzheimer's was a slowly progressing disease." They talked for a while, then her mother hung up. Her face looked as if she'd been hit.

"What did he say?" Jen asked. "Why is Daddy so bad?"

"The doctor said that sometimes with early onset, the disease can suddenly accelerate." She shook her head. "No! It can't happen this way!" she cried and ran from the room. Jen started to follow. "Please, Jen, I need to be alone. Go see if your father's all right."

Every day when Jen got home from school, she would find her father pacing the house, wandering from room to room. His face would light up as soon as he saw her. "Jenny! There you are. What time is it?"

"Three-thirty."

"Where have you been all day?"

"At school, Daddy."

And the next afternoon it would be exactly the same, with exactly the same questions.

Jen remembered the nurse's suggestion about a schedule. Each day after school, she would fix them both a snack. Then they'd swim or sit in the hot tub if her dad seemed more agitated than usual. On weekends she would take him to the park early in the morning when no one would see them. They'd knock the ball back and forth across the net.

Jen's dad seemed to be better with her than with her mother or even Rosita. Maybe it was because she never had to give him orders. But as each day passed, Jen found it harder and harder to find ways to keep him busy and entertained.

Sometimes her father would refuse to eat. Other times, he would keep repeating, "Where's my dinner? Isn't anybody going to fix dinner?"

One morning, after the dozenth question about dinner, Jen's mother blew up. "David! It's not dinner time. Can't you remember anything?" She burst into tears and ran from the room.

Jen's father sank down into the rocker and slowly began to rock. He had taken to carrying the crystal paperweight around with him, rubbing and twisting it between his fingers. His rocking picked up speed. The squeaking of the rocker was irritating as it went faster and faster. . . .

"Daddy!" She crossed to the back of the chair and held it so he couldn't rock. "Please, don't rock any more. How about a peanut butter and jelly sandwich?" she asked, trying to get his mind on something else.

"Sounds good. I'll get out the—uh—what

did you just say?"

"Peanut butter and jelly," Jen repeated.

"That's it. I'd like that."

Jen made the sandwiches and handed her father one. He had just finished his when Jen's mother came back to the kitchen.

Jen's father looked at her mother's red eyes. "Ellie, is there something wrong?" he asked. "You've been crying. I can always tell."

"I'm sorry, David, I didn't mean to yell."

"Yell?"

"Never mind." She took a long quivering sigh, then smiled weakly and kissed his cheek. "I'm just kind of tired. It seems as if everything in the world has gone wrong with my play. One of the cast members has mumps, and he's in practically every scene."

"What play is that?" he asked. "Jenny, where's my dinner. I haven't had a bite to eat today."

"Daddy, you just ate a—" She heard the impatient tone of her voice and stopped. "I'll fix another sandwich."

Jen made up her mind right then and there to go to the support group meeting the next week. Maybe somebody in the group could tell her how to keep from getting cross with her father. She told her mother her plans.

"Come with me, Mom."

"I don't want to talk about our problems to a bunch of strangers," Jen's mother said. "What good would it do? But I'll take you if you want to go."

☆　☆　☆　☆　☆

On the tenth of October Mrs. Burke drove Jen to the support group meeting. It was at a local savings and loan. "I'll wait out here in the car," her mother said.

Jen found the proper room. She hesitated in the doorway. There must have been eight or nine teenagers sitting at a long table. Mom was right, she thought, I don't want to talk about Daddy in front of these kids. She started to leave, but a woman seated at the head of the table saw her.

"If you're looking for the Alzheimer's Teen Group, you're in the right place. Come on in. We haven't started yet." She motioned to an empty seat.

The faces were a blur as Jen sat down.

"Hi, Jennifer."

She jerked her head up, surprised that anyone knew her name. She looked across the table, and her heart sank. There sat Gary, smiling at her.

Ten

JEN wanted to sink through the floor. She had never dreamed she would see someone she knew. And then to have that someone be Gary Sivert—how could fate be so cruel? It was bad enough that Caroline and the other kids at school knew something was wrong with her father, but she hated the idea of Gary knowing.

Avoiding his eyes, she mumbled, "Hello."

She signed her first name and phone number on the sheet of paper that was passed around. She barely heard the woman in charge introducing herself as Mrs. Andrews, a social worker. Then it hit Jen. What was Gary doing here? Of course, she thought, his grandfather, the one he has to take care of all the time, must have Alzheimer's.

"This is the first meeting of teens," Mrs. Andrews was saying. "If you all think it's worthwhile, we'll schedule more meetings."

Jen tried to concentrate on the woman's words as she began giving them a little background on Alzheimer's Disease.

"From now on, we'll call it AD. It doesn't sound quite so ominous, does it? You all need to understand that the person with AD acts the way he does because he's sick. He has no control over his actions. Some of you probably feel very mixed up. Part of you loves the person who's sick, but another part of you may wish he weren't there."

"Yeah," one boy said. "I had to give up my room to my grandpa. I don't mind that so much, but whenever I'm watching TV, he comes in and turns off the set."

They went around the table, each person saying what bothered him or her.

"I can't play my stereo," a girl said. "I can't make any noise in the house. I don't even want to come home from school anymore."

"My folks yell at me all the time now."

"Mine argue all the time."

"Sometimes I get mad at my granddad. I hollered at him once. He started to cry, and I wanted to cut out my tongue."

"My grandpa is so messy. I don't like to eat with the family anymore. He slurps his soup and spills half his food down his front. And guess who has to clean up the mess on the floor?"

"I love my grandma, but she—does things. Mom takes her with us to buy groceries and Grandma stops to talk to everybody in the store. She tells people all these personal things. I mean, it's really embarrassing."

"You want to talk about embarrassing. My grandfather has to wear diapers! Boy, I never thought I'd be sitting around a table with other kids and telling them my grandpa wears diapers!"

Everyone started to laugh, then stopped, embarrassed.

"Don't be afraid to laugh at your problems," Mrs. Andrews said. "Don't be afraid to have fun. It helps if you and your family can keep a sense of humor. Now, does anyone else have something to share?"

Gary spoke up then. His voice was low. "I feel so helpless."

"It's perfectly normal for all of you to feel the way you do. You're embarrassed, guilty, angry, frustrated, and helpless. You can't change the situation, but you can change how you react to the problems. Don't hate yourself if you get impatient or get mad and yell. Go punch a pillow or run around the block. You're all human. Anyway, chances are, your grandparent won't even remember it the next day. No matter how hateful a person with AD may seem, just keep one thing in mind. It's not the person talking—it's the disease."

Mrs. Andrews looked around the table, then glanced at the sheet of paper everyone had signed. "Jennifer, we haven't heard from you. Is there anything you can share with us?"

Jen didn't say anything for a bit, then in a choked voice she said, "I'm afraid my dad is going to—to die."

☆　☆　☆　☆　☆

After the meeting, Gary drew Jen to one side. "I'm so sorry, Jennifer. I knew something was going on with your dad, but I never dreamed it was AD."

Jen nodded, unable to speak.

"Boy, it must be doubly terrible for someone young like him. Look, if there's any way I can help, you ask. Okay?"

"Okay," she said. She had thought she'd feel more embarrassed, but, somehow, it helped that they shared something. "I guess I'd better go. Mom's waiting outside."

"How come she didn't go to the adult group?"

Jen picked her words carefully. She didn't

want to sound as if she were criticizing her mother. "I don't think she's really accepted the fact that daddy has AD."

"My dad was the same way. But the meetings have helped him."

"Yeah. I couldn't believe it. I've felt exactly the same way as most of the kids in our group."

"Now I know why you kept turning me down," he said. "I was beginning to think I had a large wart on my nose or something."

Jen smiled faintly. "Me, too—when you didn't come to my party."

"Now that we both understand, how about playing some tennis in the morning?"

"I'd like that. Mom is taking Dad to buy some clothes without buttons or zippers. Is eight o'clock okay?"

Gary agreed. He wanted to take her out to the car, but Jen asked him not to. "Mom might feel funny seeing somebody she knows."

They waved, and Jen hurried out to the parking lot.

"Well, how was it?" her mother asked. "Pretty dreary?"

"No, it was helpful. You ought to go." Jen saw the grim line to her mother's mouth and didn't argue. "Did you get tired of waiting?"

"No. As a matter of fact I managed to get

some work done." She pointed to the notebook on the seat. "I was jotting down ideas for a new play."

"About Alzheimer's Disease?"

"No, it will be about a girl whose friend is killed by a drunk driver. It must be terrible to lose someone you love that way. It's so senseless."

Maybe it's worse to lose someone you love in bits and pieces, Jen thought. Maybe it's worse to have to watch them become someone you hardly know.

☆　☆　☆　☆　☆

The next morning Jen awakened with a new feeling of freedom. She was actually going to do something just for fun. But then a twinge of guilt gnawed at her stomach for the selfish thought.

Before she could change her mind, she hurried to the park. Gary met her at the gate.

"I was afraid you'd change your mind," he said.

"I almost did, but how did you know?"

"I've been through it. Remember? I felt guilty every time I left my grandma alone with my grandpa. I have an idea. After we play a set or two, how about coming back home with me? It's not too far," Gary said.

"Oh, I don't know. How bad is your grandfather?"

"He doesn't remember any of us much anymore. He wanders outside sometimes. And he can't control himself—you know?"

She nodded. "I just don't think I want to see what my dad will look like someday."

"Please. Just come for a few minutes. I want you to meet my grandmother. She's pretty special."

Jen finally agreed. They were both a bit rusty at tennis and only played one set before they went to Gary's house.

He lived about ten blocks away on a street lined with pepper trees. Every third house was alike.

Gary's parents had left for the insurance office. His grandmother was sitting on a couch by the window, knitting a sweater. She looked up and smiled. Jen could see where Gary's nice smile had come from.

"Hi, Grandma, I want you to meet my friend, Jennifer Burke. My grandmother, Mrs. Sivert."

Mrs. Sivert held out her hand. Jen took it, and the old lady placed her other hand over Jen's. "I'm glad you came to visit, my dear. Gary's talked about you," she said.

"Really?" Jen glanced at Gary. He turned red and shrugged.

Gary's grandmother must have been very pretty when she was young, Jen thought. All the lines in her face turned up as if she smiled a lot.

"Did you have any trouble with Grandpa?" Gary asked.

"No. But he's restless today. I expect he's in the bedroom now."

"I'll just take a look to see if he's okay," Gary said. "Jennifer, do you want to see the rest of the house?"

"Sure." She followed Gary through the large living room. The decor was modern, but the house had a strangely bare look. Then Jen realized that there were no knickknacks around.

"You're place is so neat," Jen said.

"It's because of Grandpa. We have latches on all the cupboards and drawers. I keep my bedroom door locked, too. Come on, I'll show you why."

They went down the hall to his room. Gary unlocked the door, and Jen looked inside. On a long desk was a computer, printer, and modem.

"One day Grandpa got in here while I was in the kitchen getting a drink of water. I'd been working on a story, so I left the computer on. Grandpa was fascinated by the green letters and began punching every button in sight. I lost about five pages of my story."

As Gary was locking the door again after them, an old man came shuffling down the corridor. His head moved from side to side as if he were hunting for something.

"Hi, Grandpa," Gary said. But the old man didn't answer. "Did you lose something?"

"I can't find her. I can't find her. I can't find her," he said in a flat monotone.

"Come on. I know where she is." Gary took the old man's arm and led him to the living room.

As soon as he saw his wife, his face brightened, and he hurried over to her.

"Come, sit down beside me," she said gently.

Without bending his knees, he dropped to the couch. Gary's grandma took his hands in hers. "I've missed you, Frank, dear."

Jen watched as Mrs. Sivert spoke slowly and lovingly to her husband. And all the time she stroked his hands. Jen could see the agitation leave the old man. After a few moments he leaned over and peered into her eyes.

"Will—you—you—you—marry me?"

"Of course I will, my darling." She kissed him. "Of course I will."

Jen wanted to cry. She swallowed hard and looked at Gary. He motioned for her to follow him.

In the kitchen, Jen sank down on a chair. "Oh, Gary, they're so sweet."

"Every day he asks her to marry him. He's forgotten they've been married for almost fifty years. He doesn't remember who she is, but somewhere deep inside he knows he loves her."

"How can she bear it?"

"In some ways it's easier now that he isn't aware of what's happened to him. He really hated it in the nursing home. One day the home called and said they couldn't keep him any longer. They said he'd go up and down the halls looking for somebody. He'd keep going into different ladies' rooms. He was trying to find Grandma."

"Gary? Do you—are you—you know— worried that you'll get it, too?"

"Sometimes. But you can't think about that. The statistics aren't very high that we'll get it. Anyway, with all the research going on now, maybe they'll soon have a cure for AD."

Jen closed her eyes. "I hope you're right, but sometimes it's hard not to be afraid."

Eleven

SOMEHOW Jen found the strength to deal with her problems. It helped to have Gary to talk to, someone who really understood. Every free minute she had, she spent with her dad. So what if her school work suffered? So what if the other kids thought she was stuck up because she wouldn't join in the school activities? Her father was more important. And after seeing Gary's grandfather, she didn't want to waste one single moment.

Jen, her mother, Rosita, and even Juan tried to keep an eye on Jen's father. But it was impossible to watch him all the time. And it was even more impossible to know what he might do.

They hid the keys to the car from Jen's dad. But one day he managed to find them. He backed the car out of the garage, and the door closed automatically. Then for some reason, he put the car in drive and hit the gas. The car plowed right through the garage door.

"David, I've asked you not to drive anymore," Jen's mother said quietly.

"I thought it was in reverse," her father said. "Anybody could make that mistake."

Jen saw the effort it took for her mother not to raise her voice. "Rosita, will you please ask Juan to remove the distributor cap until I can sell the car."

Jen's father blinked rapidly. He tilted back his head as if that might keep the tears from running down his face. "I"—he swallowed—"I never really dreamed it would come to this. Ellie, I'm sorry I'm such a burden to you and Jenny."

Jen turned away so she couldn't see her father's hurt face. She kept telling herself over and over, he won't remember this tomorrow.

Jen thought her dad often seemed very depressed, yet sometimes he was his old self. Jen would help him make popcorn, and they would all sit around watching a musical show on TV. Her dad would get out his guitar and play. Jen was glad he hadn't lost that skill yet.

He seemed to have lost his sense of time, though. He marked off the days on the calendar as he had always done. But he wasn't even aware that they hadn't celebrated his birthday or Thanksgiving. Jen's mother just wasn't up to it. She had even asked Jen's grandparents not to come out for their usual winter vacation.

But Christmas was different. It was her dad's favorite holiday. We have to celebrate Christmas, Jen thought. But there was only a week left to make plans. Jen caught her mother in the driveway just as she was leaving for work.

"Mom, wait up." Jen hugged her arms in the cold. "Aren't we going to put up a tree and decorate the house?"

"Not this year, honey. I just can't handle it."

"But Rosita and Juan and I can do everything. Please," she pleaded. "You know how much it means to Daddy. Maybe it will help him remember things. The social worker at the support group said we should try to encourage him to use his mind."

"All right. Maybe it would help. But we can't spend much money this year."

"I thought you said we didn't have to worry."

"Well, I was wrong. Your dad's always taken care of the bills. I had no idea how much everything costs."

"We could buy a little tree. And you don't have to get me any presents."

She sighed and gave Jen a tired smile. "Go ahead and get Juan to put up a tree. But I'm going to have to work late nearly every night next week. You'll have to do most of the work. Now get inside before you freeze."

Jen ran into the kitchen. "Rosita! Rosita! We're going to have a Christmas, just like always."

The next few days Jen and Rosita were busy making gifts and baking cookies. They cut out cookies shaped like candy canes and Santas and animals. One day Jen's father wandered into the kitchen while they were baking. "Mmm, smells good in here. Are you making my gingerbread boy?" he asked.

Every year Rosita made a huge gingerbread boy and decorated it with frosting and raisins. "It's in the oven now, Senor David."

Jen was at the table decorating a candy cane cookie. He wandered over and stuck his finger in the red frosting and then licked his finger. "Mama used to make me a gingerbread boy. She let me put on the buttons and eyes."

Jen and Rosita looked at each other. He had always said he didn't remember his mother or father.

"That's the nice thing about Christmas, Senor David," Rosita said softly. "It brings back the good memories of childhood."

She took the cookie sheet out of the oven and carefully slid the huge cookie onto the wax paper on the table. Jen waited for the cookie to cool, then spread on the frosting. Her father was watching closely.

"Daddy, would you like to put on his buttons?"

"Oh, yes. He has to have six buttons." He reached for the bowl of raisins and began counting them out. "One—two—three—f— five—seven—" He stopped and frowned.

"One more and you have six," Jen said.

He took one raisin and very carefully put it in place. But the second one wouldn't go where he wanted and he angrily pushed it into the soft cookie. The gingerbread boy broke in half.

"I didn't mean to break it. Honest I didn't."

"Daddy, it's okay. We can stick him together again with frosting."

Her father was sitting hunched forward, twisting his hands and making little hurt cries.

Quickly, Jen repaired the damage. "See, he's just like new."

Her father's smile of pleasure was almost more than Jen could bear.

"I'll take care of the cookies," Rosita said to Jen. "Why don't you go ahead and start bringing down some of the decorations."

Jen headed for the attic. It was a wonderfully musty, mysterious place. When she was younger, she and Caroline used to go there and play dress-up.

Jen made several trips up and down the stairs. After the fifth load, she decided to rest for a bit. She sat on an old rocking horse, thinking about how much fun she'd had when she was little. There were so many good memories.

Jen noticed some old photograph albums on a trunk and climbed off the wooden horse to look through them. Several of the albums were very old. They had pictures of her mother's family. In one she found pictures of herself as a little girl. Another was filled with pictures of her mom and dad when they were very young. She put the albums on top of a box of Christmas lights and carried them downstairs.

As she passed the family room, she heard her father laughing at an old Bugs Bunny cartoon. The only things he watched anymore were cartoons, sports, and musical shows. But the minute a commercial would come on, he'd turn the television off and wander away.

Jen set the box of Christmas things in the living room. She took the albums to her father. "Daddy, look what I found."

She opened the one with pictures of her.

"Remember the Christmas you bought me my first life-sized baby doll? See, there she is, Betsy Bumpsy."

"Terrible name," he said, but he was smiling as he turned the pages.

Jen wished she'd thought of the albums sooner.

Her dad pointed to a picture of himself dressed as Santa Claus. Jen was dressed as a marionette in the photo. Every year she and her father had performed at the children's hospital. . . until this Christmas.

"Come help us," Rosita called from the living room.

Jen left her father happily looking at the albums.

Juan had set up a small pine tree. Usually they had a huge fir that almost touched the beamed ceilings. Juan was stringing the lights. Rosita was holding one end to keep them from tangling.

"Jen, will you take that other strand and plug it in to see if all the lights are working?"

She did as Rosita asked, then she helped put on the tinsel and ornaments. When the last silver icicle was in place and the angel was perched on top, they all stood back to admire the tree. "It's beautiful," Jen said. "Who needs such a big tree, anyway?"

"Help me, Jenny."

She turned to see her father coming down the stairs.

"Oh, no!" Jen cried, then burst into laughter.

She realized she had left the attic door unlocked. Her father found his Santa Claus suit, but he hadn't been able to get the pillow in right. He looked like a Santa with a huge red growth on his hip.

He was holding out the beard. "Jenny, I can't get this on."

Juan helped him adjust the pillow. Jen got out the makeup kit and fixed the beard and mustache. She gave him rosy cheeks and a pink nose. "You look great, Daddy. I wish we could perform at the hospital like always."

Just then the front door chimed. "That must be the Woodrow children," Rosita said. "I told their grandmother to send them over for some cookies."

Jen opened the door. "Come on in, kids. Did you come over for some more swimming lessons?"

They giggled. "You know it's too cold to go swimming today," the six-year-old said.

"Oh, then I'll bet I know what you're here for. Hang on, and I'll see if I can find some cookies with your names on—"

"Santa Claus! Santa Claus!" the four-year-old squealed.

"Ho, ho, ho." Her father sat in his big chair and patted his knee. "Come on over here and tell Santa what you want for Christmas."

"That's really your dad," the seven-year-old boy whispered to Jen.

"I know, but don't spoil it for your sisters." Or for Daddy, either, Jen thought.

On impulse, Jen ran to the attic and got out her marionette costume. She quickly dressed and made up her face. Maybe they couldn't give their usual Christmas performance at the hospital, but they could do it for these three little kids.

Jen waited until her father had finished listening to the children's long gift list. Then she sank down in a heap in the archway. In a tiny squeaky voice, she called, "Santa Claus, I can't walk."

Jen held her breath, hoping her dad hadn't forgotten their routine.

"You children sit on the—uh—over there." Her father pointed to the sofa. "I think one of my toys is in trouble. And none of my elves are around."

He came over to Jen and picked up the marionette controller. Strings from the controller were attached to the neck, arms, and legs of Jen's costume.

"I can't walk," Jen squeaked again.

Her dad pulled up on the control, and Jen slowly got to her feet. One leg gave way, and she slumped sideways. Again he pulled her up. As she stood there on wobbly legs, the children clapped. Rosita and Juan applauded loudly.

Without a hitch, they went through their routine of dancing and singing. The children's faces showed their delight.

"Oh, Daddy, you were wonderful," Jen said. "You remembered every bit of our old act."

Forgetting the strings, Jen turned to fling her arms around her father. Two strings wound around his neck. He tried to move, and the strings on her legs caught him. She and her dad became hopelessly entangled. The children giggled. Rosita and Juan were grinning broadly at the predicament.

Jen's father grinned, then began to laugh.

His laughter was so contagious, Jen found herself laughing, too. And it felt wonderful.

"Oh, Daddy, I love you."

Twelve

ON Christmas morning, Jen sat on the floor amidst empty boxes and torn wrapping paper and ribbons. Rosita and Juan had given her a knitted scarf and cap. Her grandparents had sent a fifty dollar check. Gary had given her a story he had written. She stroked the velvety velour of the pink jogging suit from her mother.

Why couldn't everything be just like it always had been? But nothing was the same. There were no paper bags with their names on them filled with crazy gifts. There was no singing of carols around the piano. There was no excitement.

Jen's father was wearing the new slippers Jen had bought him. He was staring into the fire and whistling in an irritating monotone.

Jen's mother looked pale and worn. "Jen, I think I'll go lie down for a while. Keep an eye on your father. Don't let him feed the fish again. He almost killed them by feeding them three times yesterday. And turn off the tree lights. Our electric bill is ridiculous."

Jen nodded. She didn't really see how a few Christmas lights would add much to the bill. But lately her mother was worried about every cent they spent.

Jen picked up the wrapping papers and stuffed them into two sacks. She handed her father one. "Daddy, help me carry these out to the trash."

He shook his head.

"Please."

"No."

"Then come with me."

"No."

Jen sighed. When he became ostinate there wasn't any use arguing, but it was hard not to. "Okay, I'll be right back."

"I want to go home."

"Daddy, you are home."

"No, no. I want to go to my home."

"I'll get dressed, and we'll go for a walk. Okay?"

"I want to go home."

She emptied the trash, then went upstairs to change into her new jogging suit.

When she came back to get her father, he

had left the living room.

"Daddy, come on," she called. "We're going for a walk."

Jen looked in the family room, the study, and the kitchen. Her father had never hidden from her before. But then she never knew what to expect next from him. She went upstairs and checked all the rooms. She peeked into her mother's room. Her mother was there, asleep.

Jen rechecked every room and closet. Then it suddenly hit her. *I didn't lock the back door when I came in.*

The pool! Jen rushed outside and almost collapsed with relief. The pool was empty. And then she noticed that the back gate was open. She hurried out to the street, but her father was nowhere in sight.

Mr. Woodrow was just leaving in his car. She ran across the lawn to catch him. "Have you seen my dad?" she asked.

"Sorry, Jen. I haven't seen him in weeks. How's he doing?"

"It's all my fault," Jen said. "I left the back door unlocked, and he's gone. If anything's happened. . . ." Her voice trailed off.

"Get in the car, and we'll see if we can find him. He hasn't been gone long, has he?"

"No, only a few minutes."

"What's he wearing?"

"Just his grey sweatsuit and slippers."

They drove slowly up and down the streets. Mr. Woodrow looked embarrassed, as if he wanted to say something. Finally, he asked, "What exactly is the matter with your dad? I know there's nothing *physically* wrong. Your mother's never told any of the neighbors."

By the way he had accented physically, Jen knew he figured it was mental. "The doctor's don't know for sure," she said, giving her standard answer.

They had made a five block circle of the area. "I don't see how he could have gotten much farther away," Mr. Woodrow said. "Maybe you'd better go home and call the police."

"Wait! What's going on up at the next street?" Jen asked.

As they drove closer, they saw a group of boys on new Christmas bicycles. They had made a circle with their bikes, and Jen's father was in the middle. He was wearing only the top of his sweatsuit, his shorts, and socks. The kids were laughing and jeering.

Mr. Woodrow parked the car, jumped out and yelled, "Don't you have anything better to do? Now, get out of here!"

Jen hurried over to her father and took his

arm. "Come on, Daddy, get in the car."

"Will you take me home?" he asked eagerly. Then he scowled. "That other girl wouldn't take me."

"We'll get you home, Dave," Mr. Woodrow said kindly. "Climb in."

He got into the front seat with no argument. "I didn't like that other girl. She was mean and wouldn't take me to see Mama. You are taking me home, aren't you?"

"Yes, but what other girl?" Jen asked, puzzled.

"She looks like you, but she's not nice. She orders me around. If she doesn't stop being so mean, I'm going to call the police. You stay away from her."

"All right, Daddy, we'll tell that other girl to go away." She avoided Mr. Woodrow's eyes and was glad he didn't ask any questions.

They pulled up in front of the house. "Need some help, Jen?"

"He's all right now. I'll just take him in the back way. I really thank you for helping me."

"No problem. I'll see if I can find the rest of his clothes. Give me a call if he—you know, if he gets violent or anything."

"He doesn't get—!" Jen bit her tongue. What was the use in trying to explain? "He'll be fine," she said. "Thanks again."

141

Jen had just started around to the back when her mother opened the front door. "David! Where have you two been? Dear heaven, where are the rest of his clothes? Get in here, both of you!"

Jen guided her father to the porch. "I'm sorry, Mom."

"Young lady, don't you dare ever leave the back door and gate wide open again. I was worried sick!"

As her father came in he kissed her mother on the cheek. "Hi, Ellie. I went home to visit Mother."

"Mother! Your mother's been dead for years! Look at you," she cried. "You're making us the laughing stock of the neighborhood!"

Jen's father backed away from her mother's anger. He skidded on the waxed floor and bumped into an end table. An antique vase of flowers crashed to the floor. Water and glass flew everywhere.

"Now, see what you've done!" Jen's mother screamed.

Jen's father cowered against the wall, like a dog who'd been beaten. "I'm sorry. I'm sorry. I'm sorry."

Jen's mother picked up the largest piece of the vase. She stood there for a moment, then threw the piece of glass on the floor. She burst into tears and ran to her husband. "Forgive me, David." Putting her arms around him, she held him close, rocking him back and forth. "Please, forgive me."

Jen's heart twisted with pain for both of them. She put her arm around her mother's shoulder. "Mom, don't hate yourself. Tomorrow, he won't even remember this."

☆ ☆ ☆ ☆ ☆

The next day Jen and her mother were fixing breakfast while her father watched TV in the family room.

"Jen, we have to make some changes. I just can't take much more," her mother said.

"I'll be more careful. I never should have left the door unlocked."

"It's not that."

"I'm sorry about your favorite vase. Maybe we could get it repaired," Jen suggested.

"Possessions don't mean as much to me as they used to. It's just—I feel as if I'm going to shatter into a million pieces. I can't sleep. I don't eat right. I have to do all the things your father used to do. We never made a decision without discussing it first. There's no one to talk to now."

You could talk to me, Jen thought. "Mom,

why don't you go to the family support group meetings? They helped me."

"Maybe I will."

"And I think we should tell all the neighbors what's wrong with Daddy."

"No! I can't do that."

"It's better than having everybody think he's crazy."

"I don't know about telling the neighbors, but I will go to the next support group meeting. And I guess we'd better get your dad that ID bracelet, too. In fact, I suppose we should do all the things that nurse told us— like putting away all the knickknacks and making the place safer. We'll do all that before you go back to school, but first you and I are going to get away."

"Away? Where away?"

"You'll see. I'll ask Rosita and Juan to stay with your father for a couple of days. And then, it'll be just the two of us on the town."

"We can't afford to go anywhere for two days."

"For this one time, I don't care how much it costs. Honey, we need each other now."

☆ ☆ ☆ ☆ ☆

The next morning, dressed in their best

clothes, Jen and her mother left the house early. Jen had no idea where they were going until her mother pulled up in front of the Beverly Hills Hotel. A doorman took their bags, an attendent drove off with the car, and Jen and her mother walked into the famous hotel.

"We are going to spoil ourselves rotten today. First we're going to get the works—a massage, a manicure, and a hairdo. I'm getting a facial, which you don't need. We're going to eat in the fanciest restaurant in town, then I have tickets for a play. I know one of the actors."

The day went by like a dream. Jen and her mother had never done any really adult things together before.

The play was a musical that Jen loved. But even better was going backstage to meet the stars of the show. Jen couldn't wait to tell Caroline.

Afterward they went to a dessert shop near the theater. They ordered the fanciest, gooiest, most scrumptious dessert on the menu.

That night, after they had talked about the play and the actors, and were pleasantly sleepy, Jen crawled into bed with her mother.

"Tomorrow, we're going to sleep in as long

as we want," her mother said. "Then we'll order room service and have breakfast in bed."

"Mom, thanks for a great time."

"Honey, I know I've been neglecting you. But I'll try to do better from now on. I can't take the place of your—" Her voice broke. "Oh, Jenny, I don't know what I'd do without you."

☆　☆　☆　☆　☆

During the next week, Jen and her mother made drastic changes in the house, both to make it safer and to save money and effort.

"Now, young lady," her mother said with mock sternness, "things are going to be different with you, too. I want you to do your homework as soon as you come home every day. You're going to practice your piano. I haven't heard you touch it in weeks. You're going to ask your friends over. And you can start right now by inviting them here tonight for a New Year's Eve Party."

"Mom, I don't want a party. It costs too much. And besides, most kids will already have plans."

"So we keep it simple—chili dogs and cole slaw. And I'll bet a lot of kids are just sitting at home wishing they could go to a party. Anyway, you can't say no, because in"—she stopped and looked at her watch—"fifteen minutes two people will be here to plan this shindig."

Jen figured it was Caroline and Mindy who were coming over. She wasn't prepared when Gary came to the door with Caroline.

"Gary!" She found herself blushing. "I wasn't expecting to—I mean—"

"As soon as you get your tang untungled, you might say hello to me, too," Caroline said. She was standing there with her hands on her hips. "Or aren't you glad to see me?"

"Oh, Caroline, yes, both of you. It's great to see you guys."

"I figured you'd let your friends know whenever you decided to come out into the world again."

"I just haven't had time. . . ."

"We understand," Gary said. "But how about asking us inside?"

"Hey, I'm sorry. Come on in."

Jen's mother came to the living room. "Hi, kids. You can use the family room to make your plans. Jen's father is asleep. I'll be in the kitchen making my world famous chili. Actually it's Rosita's famous chili. I'm just thawing it out."

Jen led her friends into the family room. She locked the door to make sure her father didn't walk in on them. "Well," she said, spreading her arms. "I guess we're going to have a party."

"I'll do the calling," Caroline said. "You and Gary pick out the record albums."

Jen looked at both of them and realized how good it felt to be with her friends again.

She opened the record cabinet. "Gary, how are your grandparents?"

"There's no change. My folks hired a part-time nurse so I could get away more. It was hard with school and basketball practice and—well, you know what it's like."

"I sure do."

"Well, why not, for Pete's sake?" they heard Caroline say on the phone. "I think you're a real jerk. Good-bye!" She slammed down the receiver.

"What's wrong?" Jen asked.

"Oh, nothing. So far, everybody's busy." She avoided Jen's eyes. "It is kind of late to invite people for tonight."

"They just don't want to come on account of my dad," Jen said softly. "That's it, isn't it?"

"I'll try Jimmy Kruger. He's a good dancer."

But it was the same with everybody.

"I thought they'd have forgotten the open

house by now," Jen said, trying to hide the hurt in her voice.

"Oh, it isn't that," Caroline said. "One of the kids saw your dad running around the streets naked and—"

"He wasn't naked! I hate that Academy and the kids. I'm going to ask Mom if I can transfer to public school."

"So who needs a bunch of kids? I'll call my friend, Steve Corbin." Gary said. "The four of us can have a good time."

"I'd better tell Mom," Jen said, and headed for the kitchen.

"Mom, you'd better not thaw out all that chili. Nobody wants to come to my party. It's all over school about Dad. You know. . . ."

She felt a hand on her shoulder and turned to look up at her father's sad face. "I'm sorry I cause you pain, Jenny. Did I do something to embarrass you?"

"Oh, Daddy, no! Never."

And she meant it. Nothing he could do would ever embarrass her again.

Thirteen

"LOOK what I have! Come on, everybody. It's show time!"

Jen's mother practically flew into the family room where Jen was watching a rerun of *Happy Days*. Jen's father was staring at the aquarium, fascinated by the bubbles and quick movements of the fish.

Jen knew by her mother's face what she was excited about. "You got the advance copy of your TV play. Right?"

"Right. Want to watch it now or after dinner?"

"After," Jen said. "I want to invite Caroline and Gary and Mindy and—"

"Jen, if you don't mind, I'd like to watch it the first time with just you and your dad. You're the two most important people in my life."

Jen was touched. "Sure, Mom. Let's watch

it right now." She turned to her father. "Come on, Daddy, we're going to see Mom's play."

"Oh, that's good." He took a seat close to the set.

Her mother slid the video tape into the VCR machine. The movie began with two teenagers in a car. It was weaving back and forth across the highway. The young driver took a drink from a bottle, just as the car entered a tunnel. There was a scream, then the sound of a crash.

Jen's father had been sitting there quietly, leaning forward, seeming to understand what was going on.

"Now, watch for the credits," her mother said.

On the screen flashed the words, "Assistant Director, Ellen H. Burke." And following that in even larger print were the words, "Screenplay by Ellen H. Burke."

Jen's father watched the credits roll, then got up and switched off the television and started to wander out of the room.

"Daddy!" Jen jumped up.

"Let him go, Jen," her mother said. "It doesn't matter." She gave a deep sigh. "For years your father has been my biggest cheerleader. He never let me give up on myself. And now—now that I can't share my success with him, it doesn't seem to mean as much."

"Mom, I'm sorry."

"I know. It's just one more thing I have to get used to."

But how do you ever get used to seeing your mother so unhappy? Jen wondered. How do you ever get used to watching your father become more and more like a child?

☆　☆　☆　☆　☆

For over two months, Jen had been practicing every day for Academy's May recital. Out of all the pianists in the music class, Mrs. Helmer had chosen her to do a solo.

This Saturday morning, she and her father were in the family room. She was having difficulty with the Saint-Saëns concerto. And her father wasn't exactly helping. He was playing "Puff the Magic Dragon" on his guitar. At least Jen thought that was what he was trying to play. The last few weeks he couldn't seem to remember the chords to any songs.

Jen started to ask him to stop, but instead, she quietly left the room and went out to the piano in the living room.

She was still struggling with the *Andante*

sostenuto when her mother came in and sat watching her. After a few minutes, Jen stopped. "Did you want me to do something?" she asked.

"No. Are you getting nervous about the recital?"

"No, not really. I'm just having trouble with one section."

Her mother nodded, but Jen knew her mind was on something else. "Mom, what's wrong?"

"Nothing. I've just been thinking. How would you like it if Grandma and Grandpa came out for your birthday and the recital?"

"Fine, but I thought you didn't want them to see Daddy."

"After talking to the members of the support group, I realize I'm not being fair. Mother and Dad should know. Anyway, I want to give them a chance to take some of the heirlooms. Jen, dear, I hate to tell you this, but we're going to have to sell the house. It's just too big. I'm so sorry. I've tried to hold out as long as I could, but. . ."

Jen got up from the piano and went to her mother. "It's okay. Honest. Can we get a house all on one floor? Going up and down these stairs a zillion times a day is getting to me."

"Absolutely. There's just one thing I'm

worried about. I've been reading those books the nurse told us about. One said that moving can be really traumatic for a person with AD."

Jen smiled to herself. Since her mother started going to the meetings, she seemed to have accepted the idea that Jen's father had Alzheimer's Disease.

"But I think if we keep the things that are important to him, maybe it won't be too hard on him," she said, sounding doubtful.

"I think it's a good idea, Mom. And I'd like to have Grandma and Grandpa come to the recital. It's been almost a year since we've seen them."

The TV in the family room blared. Her father had pushed the wrong buttons again. Jen got up to go turn it down before the neighbors complained.

"I'll go, Jen. You get back to that piano. You have only two weeks to get that concerto perfect."

Only two weeks! Now, I am nervous, she thought.

The two weeks seemed to fly past. Her grandparents were to arrive the day before the recital. At the last minute her mother wasn't able to go to the airport to meet them. So her grandma and grandpa had to take an airport limousine, then a taxi. They weren't in a very good humor when Jen met them at the front door.

"Hi, Grandma. Grandpa. Come on in."

Jen's grandmother presented her cheek to be kissed. Then she drew back and looked around the living room. "What in the world! Are you having the floors redone?"

Jen had become so used to the bare, unwaxed floors that she hadn't realized how it must look to them. "No, we—"

"Where are the lamps and vases and figurines?" her grandmother demanded.

"They're put away. Mom will explain when she gets here." Jen looked at her watch, wishing her mother would walk in that minute. "Do you want to take your bags upstairs and freshen up?" Jen asked. "Maybe you'd like to take a nap after that long flight."

Jen's father was outside helping Juan water the plants. Jen didn't want her grandparents to see her father until her mother was there.

"No, Jen, we don't need a nap." Her grandmother dabbed at her forehead with a tissue. "It's so hot out here in California. What I'd really like is something cold to drink."

"Would you like a drink, too, Grandpa?"

"Nothing for me, thanks, I'll take the bags

up," Jen's grandfather said. "Same room?"

"Same room." He was halfway up the stairs before Jen remembered the gate. They had put a small gate at the top to keep her father from falling down the stairs at night. *Mom, please get home.*

In the kitchen Jen fixed a glass of iced tea. "I'm glad you and Grandpa could come out to visit," Jen said.

"Well, your mother absolutely insisted, not that we didn't want to be here for your birthday and program, dear," she said quickly. "But we had to change all of our vacation plans." She took a sip of iced tea, and looked intently at Jen. "First, your mother doesn't want us to come out for the holidays, and now she suddenly wants us here. What's going on?"

"Mom will tell you all about it."

Jen's grandmother turned to the patio door and looked out at the garden and yard. "This really is a lovely place. But you'd better tell Juan he's overwatering the roses."

It wasn't Juan who overwatered the plants. Her father practically drowned everything— including the cement walks, the neighbor's grass, and even the hot tub.

Her grandmother moved closer to the glass doors and peered out. "Isn't that David pulling weeds over there by the fence?"

Mom, please get home. Please.

"Yes, it's Daddy."

"Then why didn't he come pick us up at the airport? He should let the gardner do the weeding, for heaven's sake."

"He's been sick. Gardening makes him feel better."

"Sick? Ellen never mentioned he was ill."

Jen heard the door to the garage. At last, she thought.

Jen's mother came in at the same time Jen's grandfather came back downstairs.

"Hello, Mother. Dad. Sorry I couldn't pick you up." She set a package on the table. "My boss called a meeting at the last minute."

"What's this about David being sick?" Jen's grandmother asked. "And what in the world are you doing to the living room?"—she looked around the kitchen—"to the whole place? It's so empty."

"Have you got a baby here?" her grandfather asked. "I haven't seen one of those gates on the stairs since Jen was a little tyke."

Jen and her mother exchanged glances. Her mother gave a resigned sigh. "I guess I might as well tell you everything."

Just then Jen's father came in the back way.

He was carrying a weeding fork. "Ellie, I'm going to plant those—whatchamacallits—those orange and yellow ones." He walked right past Jen's grandparents to the sink and washed his muddy hands.

"David?" Jen's mother said to get her husband's attention. "Mom and Dad just got here," she told him.

Jen's father turned and looked blankly at Jen's grandparents. "It's nice to see you. Do you like to garden?" Jen's grandparents were staring at her father as if he'd just walked out of a flying saucer. "Come out and see my iris," he said. "Biggest blooms—"

"David, dear, why don't you take the weeding fork back outside?"

"Ellen, what's wrong with him?" her grandmother asked. "He acts as if he doesn't even know us."

Her mother frowned and made a motion not to say any more. "Go on, David. Take the weeding fork to Juan. He needs it."

Jen's mother's voice was full of pain and such sadness that Jen wanted to cry.

Jen's father nodded obediantly. "Glad to meet you, folks. I'd like to stay and talk, but I have a lot of work to do."

They watched him leave and go outside. Jen tried to look at him through her grandparents's shocked eyes. He had changed so much since last summer. Even physically, he was thinner and somehow, more frail looking.

"All right," Jen's grandmother said. "What's wrong with David?"

"He has Alzheimer's Disease."

"That's ridiculous," her grandmother said. "I've read about it. He's too young a man."

"I didn't want to admit he had it, either," Jen's mother said.

"Why didn't you tell us?" her grandmother wanted to know.

"I knew something was wrong when you were here last summer. You kept saying he looked just fine, and I so wanted to believe you were right. But he just got worse."

She went on to tell them how the disease had progressed. Her grandparents sat there stunned.

"Oh, Ellen, how awful for you and Jennifer," her grandmother said finally.

"What can we do to help?" her grandfather asked.

"Just try to understand. I've decided to sell the house and many of the antiques."

"You can't! They've been in our family for years and years."

"Mom, David has been retired since last summer. I need the money."

"We can help out," her grandfather said.

"No. I do thank you, but it's not just the money. It's very difficult to care for him here."

"He should be in a nursing home," her grandmother said.

"Maybe someday he'll have to go to one, but not until it's absolutely necessary."

Jen's grandmother was looking at her. "And what about Jennifer? She shouldn't be here. Jennifer, you'll come home with us this summer."

"Mom, I don't want to go anywhere," Jen said. "Grandma, I'm good at taking care of Daddy."

"I could never have gone through this without Jen," her mother said. She put her arm around her daughter. "Jen may only be fourteen next week, but she's been more adult about this than I have. Oh, Jen, I nearly forgot. Open the packages on the table—the big box first. It's an early birthday present. Try it on in case it needs any alteration."

Jen quickly opened the box and pushed aside the tissue paper. She lifted out a pale blue dress and held it up to herself. "A long dress! Mom, it's beautiful."

"I thought you'd like to wear it to the recital. I checked with Mrs. Helmer, and she said a long dress was appropriate."

Even with the hems taken down, all of Jen's old dresses were too short. She had borrowed a white dress from Caroline's sister Betty to wear the next night, but is wasn't nearly as pretty as this one.

"Try the new shoes. I hope your feet haven't grown another inch."

"Mom, thanks, but you shouldn't have spent the money. How many places can I wear a long dress?"

"How can you two be talking about long dresses and recitals at a time like this!" her grandmother cried.

"Mother, our lives have to go on."

"I don't understand any of this," Jen's grandmother said. "I'm going upstairs and lie down."

"Dinner's at five. We try to eat early when we can, because David seems to get worse in the evenings."

"I don't think I care to eat, Ellen. I don't feel very well."

"You'd better get better in a hurry, Grandma. My recital's tomorrow night."

☆ ☆ ☆ ☆ ☆

All the next day Jen had a case of nerves. She thought it would never be six-thirty. By six-fifteen she was dressed and ready to leave. She went down to the family room to show off her new dress. "How do I look?"

"Wonderful," her mother said. "The dress fits perfectly."

"You look as pretty as your mother did at graduation," her grandfather told her.

"I can't get over how grown-up you look," her grandmother said.

"Mom, before I go, do you want me to help you get Dad ready?" Jen asked.

"Ready for what?" her father asked. He was standing in the doorway. "Are we going to see Mama?"

"Surely you're not taking him tonight!" Jen's grandmother said.

"Aren't we going home?" Jen's father glared at everyone. "I want to go home."

"Ellen, are you crazy? He'll embarrass us all!"

"Grandma, don't talk about him as if he weren't here!" Jen said, not even trying to hide her anger. "He's not a two-year-old. He's a man!"

"Jen, don't talk to your grandmother like that," her mother said.

"But it's my recital." Jen had performed plenty of times with her father, but never alone before. "I want Daddy there. And he'll enjoy the program, won't you Daddy?"

"Are we putting on a show for the hospital?" her father asked. "Which act, kitten?"

"No, David," her mother said. "We're all going to see Jen play a piano solo."

"Oh, I'd like that. Is it time to go?"

"In a little bit. Right now, you have to get dressed in your best clothes."

A horn sounded from outside. "That's Caroline and her mom. Caroline's an usher. We have to be there early." Jen kissed them all good-bye. "Wish me luck."

At the auditorium, Mrs. Helmer gave the performers last minute instructions. She had chosen a nice mix of popular music, classical, and even a rock band to end the evening on an upbeat. Jen was scheduled to play after a singer and just before the band. It was awful waiting in the wings. She hardly heard the other performers. She was too nervous.

The singer, looking scared and dry-mouthed, passed Jen, took her place on the stage, and began to sing. Jen was peeking through the wing curtains at the audience. She had invited Gary and his family, and they were sitting just behind her own family.

The singer hit the last note. Jen took a long deep breath to quiet her stomach. *I'm next.*

Please don't let me hit any clunkers.

The audience applauded warmly for the singer. Then came Mrs. Helmer's introduction. "Next you'll hear Miss Jennifer Burke playing from Saint-Saëns's Concerto Number 2 in G minor, Opus 22.

It seemed like a mile from the wings to the piano. But as soon as Jen sat down at the piano and touched the keys, the butterflies disappeared. Nodding to the audience, she began to play. As always, she forgot everything except the music. She was feeling good, because she knew she was playing well. Then suddenly she heard loud whispering in the audience.

She looked out over the blur of faces and realized what the buzz of noise was about. Her father was heading up the steps to the stage.

The world seemed to stop. There was no sound except her wildly beating heart. Jen couldn't move. She couldn't speak. Her father picked up one of the guitars from the band and walked over to the piano. Mrs. Helmer's pale face peered from the wings. Jen saw her mother start after her father. But she stopped on the steps.

Daddy, no! her mind cried.

He smiled broadly and bowed to the audience as he always used to do. "Ready, kitten?" he whispered.

And then she remembered. When she was five or six and could only play a few bars of any classical song, her father would break in and they would switch to "You Ain't Nothin But a Hound Dog." They hadn't done the routine in years.

She nodded numbly. "I'm ready, Daddy."

Blindly, she played the Chopin polonaise. When her father went into the Elvis impersonation, the audience laughed appreciatively. But after the first fews bars he began to hit wrong notes. He stumbled over the words and kept repeating, "You ain't nothin', you ain't nothin'," over and over.

Just as at the open house, the laughs became embarrassed snickers. Then someone yelled, "Give him the gong!"

Jen jumped up and went to her father's side. "Stop it! Don't you dare laugh at my father!"

Don't cry. Don't let me cry.

Jen looked up at her father's bewildered face. Taking his hand, she squeezed it gently. "It's okay, Daddy. It's okay." She drew him out to the apron of the stage. There wasn't a sound in the auditorium.

Jennifer stood there looking at the audience for a long moment. Then she took a deep breath. "A lot of you know my father. And you know that he is—was—a respected lawyer. Some of you have seen him perform at hospitals and charity shows. But none of you know that he has Alzheimer's Disease. It's a terrible disease that destroys the memory." She blinked back the tears that threatened. "Well—now, he doesn't remember things much anymore." Her voice broke, and she squeezed her father's hand again. "He says— he says it's like an eclipse of the moon. The blackness is slowly devouring his mind.

"Well, my dad thought we were doing an act we used to perform when I was little." Tears were running down her cheeks, now. She could hardly get the words out. "I—I think it was the best performance he's ever given. And I'm so proud of him."

For a moment there was silence, then the audience began to clap loudly. Her mother was standing on the steps crying unashamedly. Her father looked pleased. He bowed and whispered, "We were a hit, kitten."

As they left the stage, Jen passed the kids in the rock band. She handed the guitar back to its owner. "I'm sorry," she said.

"Hey, that's okay. But man, oh man," he said, "you're going to be one tough act to follow."

Fourteen

"JEN, guess what!"

Caroline's voice on the phone fairly squeaked with excitement. Jen, who had been in her room packing, stretched out on the bed. "You're getting married tomorrow."

"Be serious. Starting on the Fourth of July, my dad is actually taking us on a three week vacation to Yosemite Park and San Francisco and a whole bunch of neat places."

"That's great. Who's us?"

"His new family and me."

"I thought you couldn't stand them."

"Oh, they're not so bad. Actually, it's kind of fun to have brothers and a sister. Anyway, I'm calling to see if you can go, too. Phyllis said it was okay."

"I'd like to, but we'll be right in the middle of moving. I'm packing up all my old games and dolls and stuff now to give away."

"I can come over later and help."

"Thanks. Gary will be here this afternoon to help pack books and records. Come on over then. And, Caroline, I think it's great you're finally going to have some fun with your dad. Bye."

Jen had to hang up fast. Her throat felt too tight to talk. She really was happy for Caroline, but it was hard not to envy her.

"Jen, will you come down and take your dad for a walk?" her mother called.

"I'll be right there."

Jen hurried downstairs to the kitchen where her mother and Rosita were sorting dishes and kitchen utensils, only keeping what was absolutely necessary.

Jen's father was rocking furiously. Ever since they'd started packing, he'd been more agitated and upset.

"David? Put your shoes on so you and Jen can go for a walk."

He suddenly stopped rocking and stared blankly at Jen. He nodded. "Hello, young lady."

Stricken, Jen looked at her mother. *"Mom!"* she said in an agonized whisper.

"It's all right, honey. He didn't recognize me this morning, either. David, this is Jenny. You remember Jenny, don't you?"

"I don't believe so," he said as if to a stranger. "Jenny. That's a very pretty name."

"Thank you," Jen said in a choked voice. "That's—that's what my father calls me."

She turned away so he couldn't see her face. *Oh, Daddy, don't forget me.* You'll never see me graduate or walk down the aisle when I get married some day. You'll never know your grandkids. Then she thought of Gary's grandparents. Mr. Sivert didn't remember his wife any more, but somewhere deep inside, he knew he loved her. Taking comfort in the thought, she straightened her shoulders, turned, and gave her father a brilliant smile.

"Shall we go on that walk now?"

☆ ☆ ☆ ☆ ☆

The movers were on a lunch break. The house, nearly empty now, echoed as Jen walked to the family room. The only things left were her piano, assorted boxes, and a few pieces of furniture.

Jen sat down at the piano. She hadn't played since the night of the recital. Maybe she'd never play again. Slowly, gently, she closed the lid.

"Jenny?"

She looked up to see her father standing in

the doorway. He had called her Jenny. Today, he knew who she was.

"Play for me."

"All right," she said and lifted the lid.

He joined her on the bench. "Jenny, play 'Yesterday, When I Was Young.'"

"Oh, Daddy, no."

"Please, honey." He rolled the crystal paperweight between his fingers, then held it up to the light. "Please play it for me, Jenny. The blackness has almost covered the moon."

She began to play the haunting song. It seemed only yesterday that her father had sung the same song on the camping trip, only yesterday when he had been so young and healthy. Tears blurred her eyes, and she could hardly see the keys.

Somehow, she managed to finish the melody. As the last plaintive note hung in the air, her father reached out and gently touched her damp cheek.

"I love you, Jenny."

If you would like more information about Alzheimer's disease or the nearest Alzheimer's Family Support Group, please contact:

Alzheimer's Disease and Related Disorders
70 East Lake Street
Chicago, Illinois 60601

Telephone: 1-800-621-0379
In Illinois: 1-800-572-0637

About the Author

ALIDA YOUNG and her husband live in the high desert of Southern California. She gets many of her story ideas while hiking in the early morning. She says there is no one around to bother her except the desert animals. Once she came eyeball to eyeball with a large coyote. They looked at each other for a long moment, then he loped off into the brush. "He wasn't scared at all."

"I've always loved novels," she says. "I think I was about ten when I decided to read every book in our library. It took me three years just to get through the *A's*. It was then I decided if I ever wrote a book I'd change my name to Aaron Aardvark so my book would be the first one on the shelf."

Mrs. Young has worked in a soda fountain, a bowling alley, a custom picture framing department, a home for old people, and in a complaint department of a large store. "I got to know many different kinds of people, and it's the people, the characters in my stories, who are important."

Other books by Alida Young include *Why Am I Too Young?* and *The Land of the Iron Dragon.*